USBORNE

Sandy Lane Stables

*More great Sandy Lane stories
for you to read:*

A Horse for the Summer

The Runaway Pony

Strangers at the Stables

The Midnight Horse

Ride by Moonlight

Horse in Danger

The Perfect Pony

Riding Holiday

Dream Pony

Susannah Leigh

USBORNE

First published in 1997 by Usborne Publishing Ltd, Usborne House,
83-85 Saffron Hill, London EC1N 8RT, England.
www.usborne.com

This is a work of fiction. The character, incidents, and dialogues are
products of the author's imagination and are not to be construed as real.
Any resemblance to actual events or persons, living or dead,
is entirely coincidental.

ISBN 978 0 7460 2490 4 (paperback)

Typeset in Times

Printed in Great Britain

Editor: Michelle Bates
Series Editor: Gaby Waters
Designer: Lucy Parris
Cover Design: Neil Francis
Map Illustrations by: John Woodcock
Cover Photograph supplied by: National Geographic

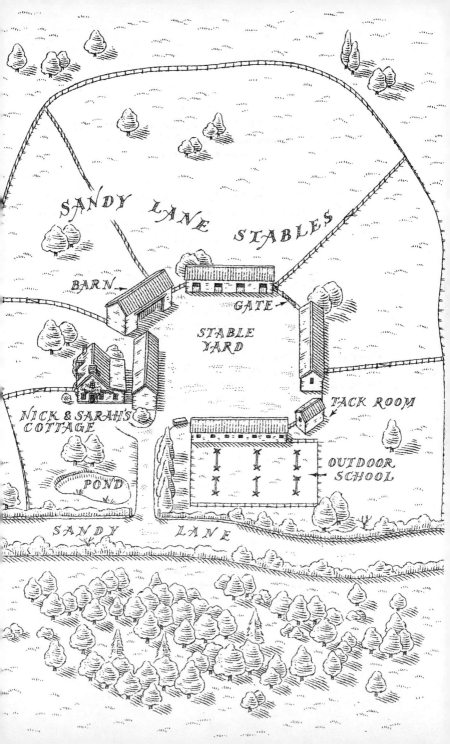

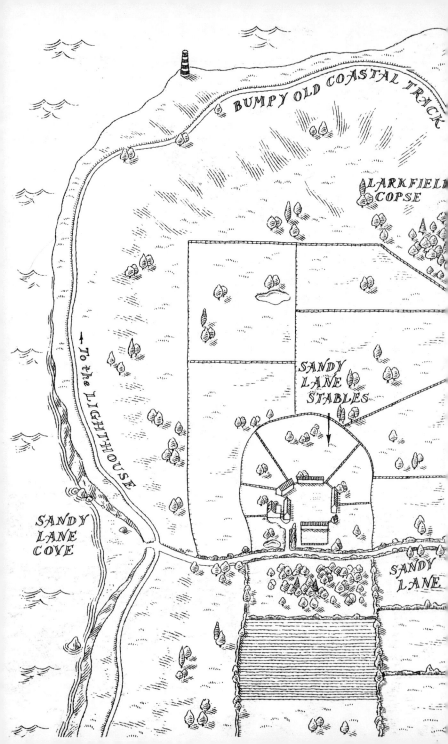

BUMPY OLD COASTAL TRACK

LARKFIELD COPSE

To the LIGHTHOUSE

SANDY LANE STABLES

SANDY LANE COVE

SANDY LANE

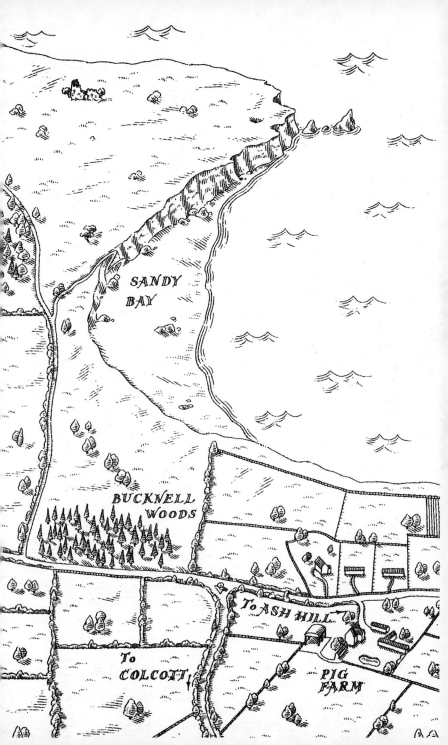

CONTENTS

1

NO RIDING TODAY

"We could play a game of cards." Rosie Edwards wrinkled her nose as she looked up from the local newspaper she had been idly skimming through.

"Boring," her friend Jess Adams answered. "Oh when will it ever stop raining?" She hunched closer to Rosie and peered through the tack room window. Outside, the rain teemed down relentlessly.

"Maybe it'll clear up this afternoon," said Rosie.

Jess gazed doubtfully out of the window at the storm clouds gathering in the darkening sky.

The two friends sat in mournful silence. They had mucked out endless boxes, filled mountains of haynets and groomed the Sandy Lane ponies till they could almost see their faces in their coats. For the moment, there was nothing else they could do.

Jess sighed. On any other Saturday, they would have been outside in the yard, tacking up the ponies for the

1

11 o'clock hack, but because of the torrential rain, Nick and Sarah Brooks, the owners of Sandy Lane, had called it off. Last Saturday's mid-morning hack had been rained off too, and Nick had got flu in the week and had to cancel lessons, so it really wasn't a good time for Sandy Lane Stables right now.

"Rain, rain, go away," Jess sang grumpily. "I'm bored, bored, bored." She crossed the room and scrabbled around in her bag.

"I was going to fill this in later," she said, pulling out a piece of paper. "But I may as well do it now."

"What is it?" Rosie looked up.

"That Browne's Department Store '*Win a Dream Pony Competition*'. I picked up a form when I was in there last week buying school shoes with my mum." Jess smiled and held it up for Rosie to look at. "What do you think my chances are of winning?" she laughed.

"Not much," Rosie admitted, grinning. "Anyway, you don't need to win a pony – not when you've got all the Sandy Lane ones. I can't imagine ever wanting to ride any other pony but Pepper."

Jess shook her head. "You're very loyal Rosie," she said. Pepper was one of Sandy Lane's oldest ponies, a stubborn little piebald who Rosie adored. "Of course all the Sandy Lane horses are great, but it doesn't make up for having one of your very own," Jess sighed.

"Well, it's a good enough close second for me," Rosie answered firmly. "Still, I suppose answering the questions would be something to do, and it's always good to test your pony knowledge. What do they want to know?"

Jess laid the piece of paper down on the desk in

front of her and, grabbing a pen, began to read the questions. "Name six points of the horse. Hmm – tendons, pastern, fetlocks, um..." She stopped and chewed her pen thoughtfully.

"Withers, croup, hocks," Rosie finished quickly.

"Pretty good," Jess said. "Hey, listen to this. 'The runners-up will win a year's supply of *New Improved Mango Miracle Shampoo*, and a bottle of *Essence of Peach Perfume*, courtesy of competition sponsors Vrai Vert Cosmetics, the Caring Cosmetics Company.' Yuk." Jess wrinkled up her nose. "Who'd want to win that? And what's a 'Caring Cosmetics Company' anyway?" she asked.

"Natural ingredients blah blah blah, environmental concerns blah blah blah." Rosie skimmed the page, reading bits aloud. "No animal testing – that's good to hear."

"It certainly is," Jess declared. "But Essence of Ponies is the only smell for me. I'm going to live in jodhpurs for the rest of my life and my hair is always going to be messy."

Rosie looked at her friend and laughed. Jess grinned back and contemplated Rosie. They couldn't look more different if they tried. Rosie was always beautifully turned out – the buttons on her jacket were never missing, there were never holes in her socks, her hair was never messy or uncombed.

Not like me, Jess thought. Strange then, that she and Rosie should be best friends. But there was one thing that bound them. They both loved horses and ponies – all shapes, all sizes. And they especially loved the horses and ponies at Sandy Lane Stables.

Sandy Lane... Jess sighed heavily as she looked

around the cosy tack room with its moth-eaten armchairs, faded but cheerful curtains, and tattered old pony magazines. This was where all the regular Sandy Lane riders congregated – a natural meeting place for Rosie and Jess and their friends Charlie and Tom, Alex and his sister Kate and, more recently, the new girl, Izzy Paterson. Only today it was just Rosie and Jess. The others in their little group were obviously far too sensible to hang around Sandy Lane in weather like this. Indeed, Rosie was only here because Jess had begged her to come.

"It might clear up. You never know," Jess had observed, optimistically.

But of course it hadn't, and although Jess knew that Nick had been right to cancel the rides this morning, the 11 o'clock hack had been the only thing that had propelled her through a dreary week of school. Still, it wouldn't have been safe to ride in the howling wind, especially with all the wet mud under foot.

"Oh no, I knew there had to be a catch," Jess groaned, coming to the end of the competition form. "The dreaded tiebreaker. Why do they always put them at the bottom? And just when you think you've finished. It's the hardest bit of the lot."

"My dream pony would be..." Rosie leaned over Jess's shoulder and read out the opening words. "Come on Jess," she said. "You can finish that in less than twenty words."

"My dream pony would be..." Jess repeated the words and paused.

Actually, having her own pony was something Jess didn't even dare dream about. It wasn't as if she would ever be able to afford one. Money was tight in Jess's

4

family. She thought of her dad and his building job. He'd already been 'rained off' a lot this winter.

Just like me today, Jess thought. But no work for her dad meant no money to spare in the family. The only way Jess was able to ride at all was by helping out at Sandy Lane in return for free lessons. Not that she minded – anything that kept her near the ponies was reward enough in itself.

"My dream pony would be one I could ride when I was awake, not just in my dreams." Jess scribbled quickly as she read the sentence aloud.

"Hey," Rosie smiled. "That's not bad, Jess. You should send it off."

"I might just do that," Jess said as she looked out of the window. "And what's more, Rosie – it's stopped raining. I think I can see the sun."

Jess stuffed the competition form in her pocket and followed Rosie happily out of the tack room, into the brightening stable yard.

2

PONIES AND RYCHESTER

Nick Brooks coughed loudly and rubbed his hands together.

"Listen up everybody," he croaked. "My throat's pretty sore so I'll keep this short."

The following Saturday had dawned bright and clear, but windy too, and the seven riders sat alert and attentive in their saddles. The 11 o'clock hack was ready to go. Rosie was on her beloved Pepper. Alex Hardy was on Hector, a huge horse of 16 hands, and his sister Kate rode the grey Arab, Feather. Charlie Marshall was on Napoleon and Tom Buchanan was riding his own horse, Chancey, a beautiful chestnut gelding. Izzy was on Midnight and today, Jess was riding Minstrel, Sandy Lane's reliable skewbald pony. The ponies shifted restlessly as an icy wind blew through the yard.

"It's been a tough winter, what with this new stables

being set up down the road and lessons here having to be cancelled," Nick continued.

The riders all shifted uncomfortably in their saddles, understanding what Nick was talking about but not really knowing what to say. The Rychester Riding Stables had been running for about a month now and already a number of Sandy Lane riders had disappeared from the books. Jess didn't like to see Nick looking so worried, but there wasn't a lot they could do about it.

"Anyway, I won't be able to take you out for a hack now – it's more important that I crack on with lessons here," Nick said briskly. "We don't want any more riders slipping into the Rychester net. However, as a thank you for all the hard work you've put in over the last few weeks, I'm happy for you to go out on your own if you want to."

"Oh, yes please!" the riders cried in unison.

"Right, well Tom's in charge. The ground's still pretty hard, so take it easy. I don't want any of you breaking your necks." Nick turned on his heels and headed off.

Tom trotted Chancey towards the gate and, one by one, the riders followed him out of the yard. As soon as they turned the corner into Sandy Lane the little group was hit by gusts of wind. The ponies' ears twitched back and forth and they flicked their tails up and down. Chancey began side-stepping and prancing around but Tom was still able to twist round and bellow above the noise.

"We'll take the coastal track up past Bucknell Woods, OK? These ponies have got the wind up, so hold on tight," he called.

Swiftly, Tom turned Chancey's head and urged him into a brisk trot. Jess followed along with the others. The rhythmic rising in the saddle, and the comforting sounds of clopping hooves and snorting ponies, competed with the noise of the wind to warm and lull Jess. She bent down and patted Minstrel's thick, shaggy neck, leaning forward to whisper in his ear.

"It's good to be out again, isn't it old boy? Don't worry, I know you're not as fit as you used to be, so we'll take it slowly. It's not a day for galloping."

Minstrel pricked up his ears and tossed his intelligent head as if he understood, and Jess remembered the times when, feeling low, she had crept into his stable and snuggled her face into his mane and told him her troubles. Somehow, he had always made her feel better.

Lost in thought, Jess had fallen a little behind the others, and now she saw them picking their way along the cliff path above Sandy Bay. There they waited for her to catch up. Giant waves thundered against the shore and sand swirled in the air as the grass in the dunes was whipped by the ferocious wind.

"Come on Jess, you slow coach..." The rest of Tom's sentence was carried off on the wind. Jess shook herself out of her dream and steered Minstrel alongside Rosie and Pepper.

"Let's get moving!"

At Tom's cry the little group guided their frisky mounts along the bumpy old coastal track.

Jess pulled in the reins and kept them short. The sound and sight of the sea had lathered the ponies into a frenzy of excitement, and the riders needed to use all their strength and skill to hold them back. As they slipped and slithered up the track's rocky incline, Jess's dreamy mood was replaced by a thrill of exhilaration, tinged with fear.

Once past Larkfield Copse, Tom suggested they stay in single file, well to the left of the path and so keep as much distance as possible between them and the cliff edge. They kept at a walk, all of them aware that to trot under these conditions would be taking too much of a risk. The horses stumbled occasionally on the bumpy frozen path, but they had calmed down a little, allowing the riders to turn their attention to the raging sea below the lighthouse. Jess had picked out a little boat, appearing and disappearing in the swell, when suddenly she felt Minstrel stiffen beneath her as if he sensed something. She looked back and noticed, just beyond Larkfield Copse, several dots haring towards them.

"Hey, look!" Jess shouted, and the other riders turned their heads and strained their eyes to see the figures. The ponies started to become restless again, but Tom held up his hand to halt the ride.

It was now obvious that what they were looking at was a group of horses and riders and, as they advanced flat out on the uneven ground, Jess could see that the horses were pure-bred beauties. At the last minute they swerved and sped past the Sandy Lane riders, right at the cliff's edge.

"Idiots. Stupid, dangerous idiots!" Tom shouted after the group of riders, holding tight onto Chancey's reins. The others were trying to calm their own ponies who were now cavorting, electrified, and trying to join in the race.

"Crazy, crazy. They are CRAZY!" Jess shouted to

the others, but secretly she couldn't help feeling a rush of admiration for the daring of the riders.

"Don't let the horses look," Tom yelled. "Turn them round. Come on, let's go."

And quickly the Sandy Lane ride set off once more, struggling to keep their ponies at a walk. The wind had changed direction now and was blowing hard in their faces. Jess was really starting to feel the cold, and her hands were so numb she could hardly keep a grip on the reins. Carefully they picked their way past the lighthouse towards Sandy Lane Cove.

"Ugh, I'm absolutely freezing, I can hardly feel my hands," Jess exclaimed, trotting Minstrel alongside Rosie. "Anyway, what was all that about? Who were those mad riders? Do you think they could be from that stables that has just been set up?"

"What? Rychester? Well, they looked completely out of control if they are," Rosie snorted.

"I suppose so," Jess agreed slowly. "But those horses were amazing weren't they? Did you notice the palomino out in front? He was superb."

"Hmm, fancy getting to ride a horse like that and being so stupid with it," Rosie replied grimly. "Uh oh, I think Tom has spotted us riding alongside each other." She nodded towards the front of the ride where Tom was staring over his shoulder, though in fact, he wasn't even looking at them, but behind them – back along the coastal track.

They turned as well and got a sudden fright. The palomino, followed closely by the rest of the wild group, was now just about on their tails. The sound of their approach had obviously been lost in the wind. They were trotting now, but Jess could see that the ponies were lathered with sweat. As they passed, a blonde-haired girl on the palomino shot Jess and Rosie a look which clearly indicated she considered them to be inferior. Then she dug her heels into her horse's side and galloped away. The rest of the ride followed at a pace. The Sandy Lane riders sat and watched quietly. Tom was the first to break the silence.

"Come on you lot," he said. "Let's go. I've seen all I want to of that crazy bunch."

The others followed his lead. But as they wound their way home along the coastal path, Jess couldn't resist stopping for just a second so she could look back at the tiny dots disappearing into the darkening sky.

****

The following Saturday, Jess and Rosie sat in the tack room at Sandy Lane, cleaning saddles and discussing the shows that were coming up. The Ash Hill Show was the next big event on the local horsy calendar.

"Of course you'll be riding at Ash Hill, Jess." Rosie's voice was reassuring, but Jess wasn't convinced.

"Don't you see Rosie?" she said. "There's absolutely no one I can enter on. Charlie will be riding Napoleon, and of course Tom will be on Chancey. I suppose Kate will enter a show class with Feather and Alex will probably go for the Working Hunter on

11

Hector. Maybe Nick would let me enter Minstrel, but he hasn't really got a chance of winning anything... oh, if only Storm Cloud wasn't lame."

"Poor old Jess," Rosie laughed as she listened to her friend's unravelling tale of woe. Jess smiled.

"Sorry, I did go on a bit," she grinned. "So tell me, what class are you down for, Rosie?"

"I'm riding Pepper in the Open Jumping," Rosie replied thoughtfully. "I bet those awful girls from the cliffs have enough ponies to ride," she added flatly.

Last Saturday's encounter with the riders at Sandy Bay had been much talked about in the stable yard. A quick check with some ex-Sandy Lane riders had told them that they had been from Rychester. Everyone had agreed that although they were a reckless bunch, the horses had looked wonderful.

"Nick isn't very pleased about Rychester being set up, is he?" Jess observed now, thinking of the beautiful palomino pony they'd seen.

"No, he's obviously rather worried about it," Rosie said. "Although how anyone could possibly want to ride anywhere other than Sandy Lane, I don't know," she added, defensively.

"Yes, but Susie Matthews and Emma James went on a Rychester hack last week and said it was brilliant," Jess remarked. "They came back full of it – how clean and smart Rychester was, how beautiful and responsive the ponies were, how they'd gone on a really fast ride..."

"How they almost broke their necks, how expensive their hack was, how they'd almost throttled a snotty girl on a palomino pony," Rosie finished, grinning.

"Maybe," Jess laughed along with her friend. "But

you must admit, Rosie, they were all pretty good riders. A bit dangerous perhaps, but certainly daring."

"Well, you've always been more adventurous than me, Jess," Rosie sighed. "Anyway, do you really think that Nick's is worried about Rychester?"

"It definitely sounds that way," Jess replied grimly.

"I suppose money's always tight here at the best of times, and with Storm Cloud being lame, Nick hasn't got as many horses to hire out as before," Rosie mused.

"That's true." Jess paused in her polishing. "And what with lessons being cancelled because of the bad weather – apparently Rychester has an indoor school, and it's full-sized!"

"Luxury!" Rosie said.

Jess looked around the scruffy tack room, and down at Minstrel's worn bridle in her hands. "You know, if I didn't love Sandy Lane so much, I'd probably think it was rather run-down."

"It's not run-down, it's just..." Rosie paused while she searched for the right words. "It's just lived-in, that's all!"

"What's lived-in?" A voice at the doorway made them jump. They whipped around to see Nick standing behind them.

"Oh nothing, Nick," Rosie blushed furiously. She wondered how much he had heard. But Nick was smiling at them.

"Well done you two." He entered the tack room and indicated the pile of tack on the table. "That needed a good clean. I think there's enough there to add up to a lesson at 2 o'clock for you both. If you want to have one that is."

"Oh yes please!" Jess and Rosie cried at once.

13

"Good. I'll see you later in the outdoor school then." Nick gave them a wave and then he was gone.

"Do you think he heard?" Jess asked as soon as he was out of earshot.

"I don't think so," Rosie reassured her. "Don't worry, Jess. I'm sure Sandy Lane isn't about to fall apart just yet. But that bridle will if you don't get some saddle soap on it!"

3

THE UNFAIRNESS OF LIFE

"So you didn't win your precious dream pony then," Jack laughed as he read the local newspaper.

"What was that?" Jess looked at her brother over the top of her horse book.

"You didn't win that competition – the one you made Mum sign the form for," Jack started again and grinned annoyingly.

"Give me that." Jess scowled, grabbing the *Daily Advertiser* out of Jack's hands.

Quickly she turned to the page Jack had been looking at and scanned the article. Sure enough, the winner of the '*Win a Dream Pony Competition*' was announced. So that was that then. Jess threw down the paper and sighed. She'd known there was no chance of winning, but a little part of her had half-hoped that she might.

Jess picked up the paper again and scrutinised the words mournfully. "Local girl, Amanda Fisher, twelve years old and now the proud owner of her dream pony..." Jess read aloud.

"Ah, the unfairness of life." Jack swallowed the last of his toast and grabbed his coat from the back of a chair. "It's a valuable lesson to learn," he said. "The Jess Adamses of this world never win the competitions. It's always the Amanda Fishers." He was out of the door before Jess had time to throw a cushion at him.

At school the next day, Rosie mentioned the competition too.

"I saw that the pony had been won by someone local. Lucky girl, whoever she is."

"Isn't she?" Jess replied. "Of course I knew I wasn't really going to win, but there was no harm in hoping."

Rosie smiled sympathetically as Jess shrugged her shoulders and moved on in the lunch queue.

"Well, yours was a good tiebreaker, Jess," Rosie said as she slid her tray along the canteen shelf and put a plate of salad on it. "Still, just think of that two hour hack Nick's got lined up for us on Saturday."

"That's true," Jess grinned, piling her plate with chips. "Things aren't so bad, are they?"

"Jess Adams!" Miss Gregory, the maths teacher, appeared at her elbow. "If I don't see your homework on my desk by the end of the lunchbreak you'll be doing it after school under my supervision."

Jess made a face at the teacher's departing back and Rosie laughed reassuringly. "Come on," she whispered. "I'll help you finish it. It's not that difficult actually."

****

16

By the time the school bell signalled the end of the day at 4 o'clock, Jess had almost forgotten about the competition. With Rosie's help, she had finished her maths homework and handed it in on time. Then they had had double English till the end of the day.

"Very good, Jess," the English teacher, Mrs. Peters, had commented, staring over Jess's shoulder at the pony doodles on Jess's pad. "I'm sure you'll make an excellent artist."

"What? Oh–" Jess reddened. "I-I–"

"Hmm, well don't let me catch you doing it again. But Mrs. Peters was smiling as she walked up to the front of the classroom.

"Sorry," Jess mumbled as she packed up her things and left the classroom, hurrying to catch the bus home.

As Jess turned down the path to the ramshackle old cottage where she lived, her mother opened the front door.

"Hurry up Jess," she called, waving the telephone receiver in her hand. "There's a phone call for you."

"Who is it?" Jess cried, flinging down her school bag in the hallway.

"Wait and see," her mother said mysteriously as she handed the receiver over to Jess.

"Hello," Jess said, a little breathless from the run.

"Is that Jess Adams?" said a friendly female voice at the other end. "Hi, I'm phoning from Browne's Department Store. You recently entered our '*Win a Dream Pony Competition*' – the one sponsored by Vrai Vert Cosmetics?"

"Yes, yes I did," Jess said, her heart beating faster as she waited for the woman to go on.

"Well, congratulations," the voice continued.

"You're now the proud owner of that pony."

"What?" Jess's heart was in her mouth. "But I-I thought someone called Amanda Fisher won it. It said so in the paper."

"She did," the woman said. "Only unfortunately what we didn't find out until today was that her parents hadn't actually given her permission to enter."

Jess's heart started to beat faster. "But didn't they sign the entry form?" she asked.

"I'm afraid that Amanda Fisher forged her mother's signature," the woman went on to explain. "And her parents don't want her to have a pony. So that disqualifies her – we cannot give her the pony if her parents don't agree. It's very sad for her, but good news for you as first runner-up. I only wish we'd found out the truth before it had gone to press."

'Good news for you.' The words rang in Jess's ear.

"Jess, are you there?" The woman started to speak again.

"Yes, yes, I'm here," Jess said, excited.

"Well, I was going to be phoning you anyway with the news that you'd won some runners-up beauty products," the woman explained. "But I'm afraid this means you won't be getting them now."

Jess almost laughed out loud. Imagine Rosie's face if she had won those! But that didn't matter. And now the woman was starting to talk again.

"Needless to say, I had a word with your mother, but it seems that her signature on your entry form was genuine, although I get the impression she was a little taken aback. Of course there's free stabling for a year at Rychester Riding Stables and the pony's tack is part of the prize too... anyway, I've popped all the details in the post. You should get them tomorrow. So, well done Jess.... Jess? Hello? Are you still there?"

Jess hadn't heard much of what the woman was saying but one word had jumped out at her – Rychester. Had she heard correctly? Had the woman really said *Rychester*? Jess stood rooted to the spot, butterflies darting and spiralling in her stomach.

"But I ride at Sandy Lane Stables," she started slowly. "Can't I keep the pony there?"

"I don't think that would be possible," the woman said. "You see the deal's already been arranged."

"But couldn't it be changed?" Jess pushed, starting to panic.

"Not at this stage, I'm afraid."

"Oh." Jess didn't know what to say. It was a dream come true to have won a pony, but to have to stable it somewhere other than Sandy Lane and worse still – Rychester!

Suddenly Jess pulled herself to her senses. She was being silly. Here she was, being handed a prize pony on a plate, and she was arguing about the stabling. How selfish of her!

"Rychester it will have to be then... yes thanks," Jess said, quick to remember her manners.

Gently her mother took the phone away from her. From what seemed like miles away Jess could hear her mother's voice, wrapping up the conversation.

"Yes, thanks for ringing. We'll wait for the details. Of course Jess will be happy to do some publicity photo-shots. Yes that would be great. Speak to you soon. Bye." And then she had put the receiver down and turned to Jess.

"Well," she said finally. "I'd never have signed that

form if I thought there was a chance you'd actually win the wretched thing. I don't know what we'll do when the year's up and the free stabling comes to an end, but I suppose we'll just have to cross that bridge when we come to it." But she was smiling, and Jess could see she wasn't cross. "We'll talk about it when Dad gets home. Are you all right, Jess?"

"All right? All right?" Jess let out a whoop of delight and flung her arms around her mother. "A pony! A pony!" she cried. "My very own pony! I can't believe it. This is the happiest day of my life. It's everything I've ever dreamed of!"

4

NO MORE SANDY LANE?

Jess read the letter through again. She had already read it twice, but it was only now as she read it a third time, that it all really sank in.

"Congratulations Jess," she read. "You are the lucky winner of the Browne's / Vrai Vert Cosmetics dream pony. Your pony will be arriving on Saturday March 1st at 11 o'clock at Rychester Riding Stables, Rychester, near Colcott, where it will be stabled for a year, free of charge. We have arranged a time for you to look around your pony's new home the Sunday before its arrival."

Then in smaller type was something about the winner giving permission for photographs and a lot of legal looking instructions. Jess didn't look too closely at that. She was too excited. She loved the bit in the letter about having won her own pony, but the words that kept jumping out at her were Rychester Riding

Stables. Would this mean she would have to leave her beloved Sandy Lane Stables behind forever? And then she couldn't help but remember Nick's worried face when he'd been telling them about Rychester. Whatever was he going to say when he heard about this?

Jess paced up and down the hallway. Maybe there was something Nick could do. Just maybe if she showed him the letter, he'd be able to persuade the competition organizers to let her stable her pony at Sandy Lane. Then everything would be perfect.

Jess turned these thoughts over in her mind as she looked at her watch. It was already half past one and she'd promised to meet Rosie at Sandy Lane at two. She'd have to be quick. Rosie would be dying to know all the details about the pony. By the time Jess had rung her the night before to tell her the news, it had been late and there hadn't been much time to talk.

****

Rosie was waiting impatiently at the tack room door when Jess cycled into the stable yard twenty minutes later.

"I can't believe it, Jess," Rosie cried at once. "You lucky thing. Come inside and tell me all about it."

Jess dumped her bike and followed her friend's excited chatter into the tack room.

"It's all thanks to you, Rosie," she said. "After all,

I'd never have sent off the competition form if you hadn't encouraged me."

"Yes, but you wrote the tiebreaker," Rosie said charitably. "Anyway, I hope you're going to let me ride this pony whenever I want to, Jess," she finished with a grin.

"Of course you can," Jess smiled with excitement at her friend. "I don't even know what the pony looks like yet," she admitted. "But I keep on imagining it. Perhaps it'll be a beautiful chestnut like Chancey. Or a black thoroughbred like Midnight."

"It might be a palomino," Rosie cried.

"I won't even care if it's a shaggy little skewbald like Minstrel," Jess smiled happily. "Whatever it's like it'll be my own pony, Rosie. My very own."

One by one, the rest of the afternoon ride piled into the room and Jess was quick to share her news.

"Your own pony?" Kate exclaimed. "Lucky, lucky you."

"I was going to enter that competition," Alex said. "I just never got around to it."

"Congratulations," Tom grinned.

And as everyone checked their names in the ride book and gathered up tack, there were more questions.

"So what's this pony like then, Jess?"

"When's it arriving?"

"Will you be jumping it at Ash Hill?"

"Just think, another pony at Sandy Lane," Rosie cried. "It's exciting for all of us."

Jess squirmed in her seat.

"Well actually, there's a bit of a problem, Rosie," Jess said, feeling uncomfortable. "You see I might not be able to stable it at Sandy Lane. It's already been arranged for the pony to be stabled somewhere else."

"Somewhere else?" The others looked on in disbelief, as if there could be no other place in the world except Sandy Lane. "Well, where then?"

"Um, it's at Rychester actually," Jess blurted the words out.

"Rychester!" Rosie was the first to speak. "Oh no Jess."

"I know." Jess hung her head sorrowfully. "They said it had all been arranged already."

"Oh." Jess's friends didn't know what to say.

"Well, it might have *seemed* like a pretty reckless stables, but perhaps it won't be so bad," Tom offered tentatively.

"And maybe the riders won't be so snooty in real life," Kate added.

But it was Rosie who openly voiced the real opinions of the others.

"Oh Jess, you can't go to Rychester," she wailed. "What about Nick?"

"Do you think I *want* to go there?" Jess interrupted her. "There's no way I want to leave Sandy Lane, Rosie. In fact, I was going to talk to Nick straight away and show him the letter... see if he can do anything about it." She made a determined face and leapt up from her chair. "I'll go and look for him now."

Jess ran across to the little cottage just behind the stables where Nick and his wife Sarah lived. The door was on the latch as usual. All the Sandy Lane riders had to do was give a quick knock and push it open. Nick and Sarah were always available and always welcoming. Jess paused in the hallway to give Ebony, the black Labrador, a pat. "Nick?" she called out.

"In the kitchen," he replied.

Nick sat at the kitchen table surrounded by paperwork. "I'm doing the accounts," he said as Jess walked in.

"Oh," Jess said, shifting from foot to foot, excitement making her unusually nervous.

"Nick, I've won a pony," she said slowly.

"A pony?" Nick's voice sounded pleased and surprised. "Well you don't look very happy about it, Jess. That's brilliant news. Congratulations, how did that happen?"

Quickly, Jess explained everything. "I know it should be perfect, it's just that there's a slight catch," she said, drawing her breath in sharply.

"A catch?" Nick looked seriously at her.

"It's the stabling," Jess hurried on. "You see it's free for a year, only I've got to keep the pony somewhere that the competition organizers have arranged, and that place is at Rychester Riding Stables."

"Rychester Riding Stables?" Nick's voice was polite and measured.

"Yes, look, it's all in this letter," Jess said handing it over. Nick started to read as Jess began to speak again.

"Only I was wondering, well hoping really, that you might phone them for me... see if we could change the stables to here. It would sound better coming from you, Nick," she said.

"Well, I don't know," Nick said doubtfully. "You see it lays out the terms and conditions quite clearly," he said, pointing to a section of the letter.

"I know." Jess looked glum.

"Look, I'll give them a ring on Monday and see what they say. They'll be closed over the weekend.

Maybe Sarah and I could even come up with something here if we could use the pony in lessons in return for stabling. Leave it with me to consider over the weekend."

"Oh thanks Nick," Jess said, relieved.

"I'm not making any promises, Jess," Nick said seriously. "So don't go pinning your hopes on anything."

"I won't," Jess said, skipping out of the door with new resolve.

Pausing by the trough in the corner of the yard, Jess looked around her at Sandy Lane Stables and sighed. The water in the small pond just in front of the cottage was muddied and cloudy. The surface in the outdoor school was worn and patchy. And one of the barn doors was hanging off its hinges. The stables looked worn and shabby, but they were clean, and Jess couldn't imagine being anywhere else.

5

RYCHESTER

Rychester Riding Stables lay a good twenty minute bike ride from Jess's house, right on the other side of Colcott. Tomorrow was Monday, when Nick would be phoning the competition organizers to see what he could do. In the meantime, there was no harm in going along with the competition letter and looking around Rychester. Jess knew though, if she was completely honest with herself, that she wasn't just at Rychester that Sunday because it had been arranged for her to look around the stables. There was something else too – Jess was curious... curious to see what the stables that was taking so much Sandy Lane custom was like.

Breathless and red-faced, Jess pedalled up the drive. A rather grand, gabled house stood a little way back from the road and beside it a wide, gravel drive swept through the gates and into the stable yard. Nervously Jess stopped her bike and looked around her. She hovered uncertainly at the end of the drive. She had arrived just as a hack was about to leave. Swinging confidently into the saddles of their beautifully turned out mounts, girls clad in immaculate riding clothes called cheerfully to one another. Jess's heart beat faster as she watched them prepare to set off.

"Dido's really lively today. I'll keep her well back," cried a girl on a delicate roan.

"Apollo's raring to go. I vote for lots of galloping!" Jess looked up with interest as the blonde-haired girl from the cliff tops called out from the saddle of her palomino pony.

"You always vote for lots of galloping, Camilla!" someone else cried. "Just keep him away from Opal."

As the ride swept past her and smartly out of the yard, Jess was horribly aware of her own dishevelled appearance. Quickly she turned her gaze to the yard.

The stable yard was lined by twelve loose boxes. Beams of bright sunlight bounced blindingly off the gleaming white walls and an Arab pony hung its head from a door and gazed at Jess. Two smart looking horse boxes in racing green were parked to the left of the stable yard, and behind them, Jess could just make out the red tiled roof of a large indoor school.

"Can I help you?" A friendly-looking girl, a few years older than Jess herself, strode towards her. Jess liked this girl's warm smile and welcoming manner immediately and at once forgot about looking smart.

"Beautiful, isn't it?" The girl smiled as she saw Jess admiring the yard. "I'm Amy Watkins, the head stable girl. Did you want to know about riding lessons?"

"Oh no. That is–" Jess paused for a second and then rushed on. "My name's Jess Adams. I've won a pony and I was asked to come and look around the stables, only I don't know if–"

But before Jess had had a chance to tell the girl that she wasn't sure if she would be keeping the pony here, the girl had started speaking. "So you're the lucky girl who's won," she smiled. "You must be so excited – it's every girl's dream to win a pony – at least it was mine. Well, feel free to look around. Your pony's arriving next week isn't she? She's going to be stabled in the loose box in the far corner."

Jess was stuck for words. Suddenly it all seemed so real. Amy knew about her pony and there was a stable already picked out for her! Jess felt a shiver of excitement run down her spine.

"Did you say 'she'?" she quizzed Amy eagerly. "Can you tell me more about my pony? Do you know what colour she is? Do you know what her name is?"

"Whoa, slow down," Amy laughed. "I'm sorry Jess, I don't know any more. They don't tell me much around here. Look, come into the office for a moment. There might be some details about your pony lying about."

She led Jess into a smart carpeted room. Charts and timetables hung from the walls, red filing cabinets lined the walls and several high-backed chairs were grouped around a big desk. Its tidyness was a far cry from Sandy Lane's muddled little tack room which doubled as an office. Amy indicated a chair and told Jess to sit down. Then she rummaged around in drawers and glanced through the papers on the walls. After a few minutes she shook her head. "Nothing here," she said.

Jess gave a little shrug.

"Poor you," Amy said, screwing up her nose in sympathy. "You must be dying to meet your pony. I'm afraid Jasper Carlisle, Rychester's owner, isn't around at the moment. He'd know more about it."   .

At that moment the phone on the desk rang. Amy answered brightly and then her voice changed. "Hello, Barry. Can you hang on a minute?" she said. She gave Jess a glance. "Look, I have to take this call," she said quickly. "Why don't you go and check out that loose box while you're here? See if it's to your liking." Amy gave a hurried wave and Jess slipped out of the office.

As Jess walked over to the corner box, she looked around her again. The sun shone brightly on the whitewashed walls, the boxes lining the yard looked smart and bright. Amy seemed really nice and friendly. Perhaps Rychester wouldn't be such a bad thing after all. Jess felt her stomach turn somersaults of excitement as she made her way to the loose box Amy had indicated.

She pulled back the well-oiled bolt on the stable door and stepped inside. The box was large and airy with white-washed walls and fresh straw scattered over the flagstone floor. A large, clean water trough was well-placed in one corner and opposite the door hung a net of good quality hay. Jess pulled the bottom door closed and leaned over it. As the sweet scent of hay rose up to meet her, a horse whinnied in the distance. Jess gazed out across the smart stable yard and suddenly Sandy Lane was forgotten. She *would* keep her pony here. She liked it. Even more than that, she was sure her pony would like it here too.

****

30

"Anyway, it had all been sorted out already... they've got a box for my pony and they're expecting us and everything. Of course it's not as nice as Sandy Lane, but there wasn't a lot I could do about it." Jess gabbled on, staring resolutely down at Nick's black riding boots. Hastily she pushed back the hair from her face and absent-mindedly fiddled with Minstrel's stirrup leather. "So I guess it would probably be better to stick with Rychester... as it's all organized," she finished lamely. She looked up now and caught Nick's eye for the first time.

"It's all right, Jess, you don't need to explain," Nick smiled kindly. "It's a good job you came back to tell me straight away – I'd have looked a bit silly if I'd called the competition organizers and arranged something and you had changed your mind. Of course we'll miss seeing you about Sandy Lane."

"Oh, but I'll be back all the time," Jess cried quickly. "I'll be bringing my pony to ride here, that's for sure."

"Glad to hear it," Nick smiled. "I hope Minstrel doesn't get too jealous." He gave the little skewbald's mane a ruffle and turned to walk back to the cottage.

When he was out of sight, Jess heaved a sigh and rested her head on Minstrel's neck. The pony shifted his weight and carried on slurping noisily from the water trough.

The sunshine, which had lasted all day, lit up this Sunday evening and left it feeling unseasonably warm. But Jess still shivered inside her jacket as she thought of her visit to Rychester. She had been so sure it was the perfect place for her pony, and yet now she did feel a little pang of guilt that she hadn't waited until Monday for Nick to phone the competition organizers.

Still, it wasn't as if she was leaving Sandy Lane for good. She wouldn't have to hang out with the Rychester riders. All this she argued to herself, and to Rosie, the next day at school.

"But the way those girls rode those poor ponies on the clifftops that day," Rosie had groaned. "How could you want to get involved with them, Jess?"

"I'm sure they're not all like that, Rosie," Jess said, trying to convince herself as much as reassure her friend. "Amy, the stable girl, is really nice and friendly."

"Well if you think Rychester is OK, then I'm sure it must be," Rosie sighed. "The main thing is that your pony's happy there."

Jess smiled at her friend. "It's not as if I'm leaving Sandy Lane for good anyway," she said. "I'm still going to come and ride with you and Pepper."

"Oh I doubt we'll be seeing you at all Jess," Rosie grinned. "Once you get sucked into smart Rychester, you'll soon forget about your old mates!"

Rosie ducked just in time to avoid Jess's flying exercise book.

6

DREAM PONY

Jess could hardly believe it – her pony was being delivered today!

"The *Daily Advertiser* will be sending a photographer along to take a picture of you and the pony for the newspaper," the lady from Browne's Department Store had said on the phone. "You need to be at Rychester for eleven."

And now it was 10 o'clock, and Jess hopped impatiently from one foot to the other as she waited for her mum to finish the ironing.

"Come on Mum!" she cried.

"Calm down, Jess," her mother laughed. "There's a whole hour to go yet."

"But by the time you've started the car and we've driven there and parked and... and... oh hurry up Mum, we can't be late!"

"All right, I'm coming," her mother said at last,

hanging up the last shirt.

Jess told herself not to get her hopes up about her pony on the car journey to Rychester Stables.

"It'll probably be an old nag," she said to herself. "It won't be beautiful. Don't dare to dream it will be beautiful – not now, when it's so close."

As the car pulled into the driveway of Rychester stables, Jess's stomach lurched with nervous anticipation and her heartbeat thudded loudly in her chest.

"I'll go and see if I can find someone," her mother said as they got out of the car. "Coming, Jess?"

"No, I think I'll just stay here," Jess squeaked as she looked anxiously back down the drive. "I don't want to miss the horse box."

"All right," her mother smiled. "Now, it's Jasper Carlisle I'm looking for, isn't it?"

"Yes, or Amy Watkins," Jess said.

Her mother walked towards the office. Jess stood in the stable yard, wishing she'd asked Rosie to come with her. But Rosie was riding at Sandy Lane this afternoon. They all would be. Alex, Kate, Charlie, Tom and Izzy would all be going out on the 11 o'clock hack. Nick would probably be taking it. On any normal Saturday Jess would have been there too. But then, this wasn't any normal Saturday.

"Hi, I'm Camilla. Do you need any help?" a strident voice rang in Jess's ears.

Jess looked up and found herself face to face with the blonde-haired girl she'd seen on the palomino pony that day on the cliff tops. She looked as self assured as she had then, but she didn't give any sign of having recognized Jess. She was closely followed by a gaggle of three girls.

"I'm waiting for my pony, actually," Jess replied quickly. "I'm going to stable it here."

"Oh another pony. Brilliant. What's it like?" Camilla asked quickly. "Is it fast? How long have you had it?"

"Um..." Jess paused. She looked hopelessly at Camilla's beautifully polished riding kit, her perfect hair, her prettily arrogant face and took a deep breath.

"I don't know yet. You see I won it in a competition."

"Oh, so *you're* the competition winner," Camilla said, laughing. "Is it your first pony?"

"Well yes," Jess admitted.

"Really?" Camilla crowed and turned to her friends. "Did you hear that everyone? This girl's won our competition pony."

Jess squirmed in her shoes and reddened.

"Well, if you need any advice on riding, you're more than welcome to come to me," Camilla offered now. "I've had my own pony for ages. He's called Apollo."

"Um, well..." Jess didn't quite know what to say. The last person in the world she felt like going to for any advice was this girl. Still, if she was going to be spending a lot of time here, she ought to try and make friends.

Jess gritted her teeth and swallowed hard. "Thanks," she said as graciously as she could bear.

But, before Jess could say any more, her mother had hurried across the yard and was talking to her. "I've had a chat to Amy," she said. "And I met a few other girls. They all seem very nice. Oh–" She caught sight of Camilla. "Have you made a new friend already, Jess? Hello, I'm Jess's mum."

Camilla smiled sweetly. "Pleased to meet you," she

said rather grandly. "Well, if there's anything Jess needs to know about Rychester, she can always ask me. I can't wait to see her pony."

"Well that's very kind of you," Jess's mum said.

"OK Jess? Feeling excited?" Amy called as she joined Jess and her mother in the stable yard.

"Hello Amy," Jess smiled. "I'm kind of nervous I suppose—" She stopped abruptly as the roar of a motor cut through the cold morning air and a horse box pulled into Rychester's drive. At last!

The driver jumped down from the cab.

"One pony care of Browne's?" he said. But Jess didn't say anything, for already the box driver was sliding back the bolts and lowering the ramp. Jess walked around to the back of the box, hardly daring to breathe. Everyone clamoured forward to get a glimpse of the pony. What would it be like? Before Jess even had a chance to look into the box, a red car had crunched into the yard.

"Which one's Jess then?" a woman asked, jumping out.

"I am," Jess said, suddenly shy.

"Jess, I'm Penny Webster from the *Daily Advertiser* and this is our photographer, Bob," she said, indicating a man by her side. "Is this your mother? Hello Mrs. Adams... nice to meet you."

But now everyone had turned back to the box. Before she could say any more, Amy's voice interrupted her. "Stand back you lot," she said. "The pony's coming down the ramp."

For a moment, Jess didn't know what to do. She closed her eyes tightly and wished and wished. "Please let it be all right," she said to herself.

She heard the driver talking. "Whoa there little pony," he said, and then she opened her eyes and saw him grab a lead rein. Walking out of the box he pulled gently.

"Come on, easy does it," he muttered and Jess gave a gasp.

There at last was her pony, stepping lightly from the box. She was small, about 13 hands. A beautiful grey mare. Her eyes were large and dark and her step was light and dainty. She sniffed the air with quivering nostrils and looked around the yard inquisitively. She seemed to take everything in. Then she stood stock still at the bottom of the ramp and gave a gentle whinny. Immediately, Jess approached her. She held out her hand and placed it firmly on the pony's velvety nose. "Hello," she said. "Hello there, pony."

The pony sniffed cautiously at Jess and nuzzled into her, pushing softly into her shoulder and nibbling gently at her jacket.

"Like her?" Penny Webster smiled across at Jess.

"Yes, oh yes," Jess breathed.

"Hmm, not bad." Camilla's voice rang loud and clear. "Not a bad little pony at all. I bet she's an excellent jumper too. I'll have a closer look at her later. I'm off on a hack now. I presume our ponies are tacked up, Amy?"

And then she left, followed closely by her gaggle of friends.

"She's a brilliant pony, Jess," Amy said brightly, as if to make up for the other girls' abrupt departure. "We'll get her settled down in her new home in no time."

"She does look lovely," Jess's mother agreed,

smiling at the pony. "And what are you going to call her, Jess?"

"I expect she's already got a name," Amy said, leafing through the pony's documents that the driver had handed to her. "I'm sure you could change it if you wanted to though. Ah, here we go, it's Skylark."

"Skylark," Jess said softly and the pony tossed her head. "It's perfect."

"Well here's to Skylark and Jess," Penny cried, breaking the spell. "Now, we need some photos. Jasper Carlisle really ought to be here – after all, it is his stables and his cosmetics company is the competition sponsor."

Jasper Carlisle owned Vrai Vert Cosmetics as well as Rychester? It was the first Jess had heard of it. Suddenly everything made sense – why she couldn't keep the pony at Sandy Lane, why the competition organizers had been so adamant she had to keep the pony at Rychester. But now Amy was talking again.

"I really don't know where Jasper's got to." She shrugged her shoulders.

"Well, we'll take a couple of photos of Jess and the pony first anyway," Penny decided.

Jess nestled in close to her new pony and beamed as Bob began to snap away. "That's great," he said. "You look very happy Jess."

"I am happy," Jess replied. "Happier than I've ever been before."

"How about a shot with Mum too?" Penny suggested.

Jess's mother came to stand next to Jess and the new pony. She lifted a tentative hand to Skylark's neck and smiled at her daughter. Bob raised his camera for the picture.

At that moment, a smart green Range Rover came roaring up the drive. Skylark started, but Jess kept a steadying hand on the lead rein. Everyone turned to stare as the car door swung open and a man in a suit climbed out. He was tall and his blond hair was slicked neatly back. Stretching out his hand, he strode towards them.

"Hi there everyone," he cried. "Apologies for being late. My meeting over-ran. No rest for the wicked, eh? Even on a Saturday. I hope I haven't missed all the excitement. Now, where's our lucky winner?"

Amy beckoned Jess towards her and put her hand on her shoulder. "Jess," she said, "I'd like you to meet Jasper Carlisle, owner of Rychester Stables and boss of Vrai Vert Cosmetics, sponsors of the competition. Jasper, this is Jess Adams, lucky owner of the new pony."

Jasper turned to Jess and beamed. "Excellent," he said. "I hope the pony is to your liking." And then, before Jess had time to reply, Jasper had turned to Penny again. "Are we going to get some photos here? Excellent. If you turn this way, you'll get the Rychester sign in the background you know."

He turned to smile at Jess again. "She's a real dream, your pony. Welcome to Rychester Jess. The finest stables in the county!"

7

DREAM JUMPER

There were a lot more photos after that. By the time Jasper was satisfied that the newspaper had taken enough, Skylark was twitching with impatience and Jess felt as though her smile was stuck to her face.

"Thank goodness that's over," Jess's mother whispered in her ear when at last the final picture had been taken and they had waved Penny off. "Most of those photos won't end up in the paper at all, but Jasper Carlisle was very insistent wasn't he?"

"I didn't realize that Vrai Vert Cosmetics and Rychester Stables were owned by the same person," Jess whispered back as she watched Jasper Carlisle disappear into the office.

"Oh, Jasper Carlisle's quite well-known around here," her mother said. "He's a renowned business man, but there's no reason why you should have known that. Still, he seems keen on animals doesn't he? This lovely stables, and his cosmetics are very natural – no animal testing I believe. Maybe you'll be able to get me some free samples, Jess? I love their *Mango Miracle Shampoo*." Her mother smiled at her.

"Honestly Mum!" Jess groaned. "I've got more important things to think about. Like getting Skylark settled for starters."

"Yes, I suppose I should leave you with your pony for a while," her mother said, glancing at her watch. "Will two hours be long enough? I'll pick you up then."

"Thanks Mum, that would be perfect," Jess replied quickly.

Seeing Mrs. Adams about to leave, Amy hurried across to Jess.

"Shall I take you over to Skylark's stable now? I'll show you where you can keep her tack and everything and explain a bit about the routine here," she offered. "Then maybe you could ride her for a little while, Jess. How about trying her in the indoor school? It's warm and quiet and you can get used to her paces in there. And she can get used to you."

"Oh yes!" Jess's eyes shone with delight. In all the excitement of Skylark's arrival, she had almost forgotten that she could actually ride her... that she was going to be able to ride her whenever she wanted. She couldn't wait to see if the pony was as perfect as she looked.

Half an hour later, tacked and mounted, Skylark circled the indoor school. Jess pushed her gently through her paces, from a walk to a rising trot to a collected canter. To her delight, the pony was responsive and alert. Her rhythm was fluid and she even changed pace effortlessly. She really was a dream to ride.

"She looks good, Jess," Amy called from the side of the school. "You've really got a lovely rhythm there."

"It's all Skylark," Jess said. "She knows just what to do."

"You're a pretty good rider too, Jess. You must remember it's not just the horse," a male voice boomed across the school. "There's no room for modest riders in my stables."

Jess brought Skylark to a halt and looked around to see who had spoken. There stood Jasper Carlisle, leaning against the rail and watching her closely. Jess blushed with pride. With Skylark going so well, Jasper must think she was a really good rider. Had Nick ever paid her a compliment like that? If he had, she couldn't remember it. Jasper went on. "You might think about using a stick on her. She's a bit slow around the corners. Still, this pony looks like she's got spirit. Why don't you try her over a few jumps. See how she goes?"

"I'll put the poles out," Amy volunteered.

"Poles?" Jasper laughed. "That's far too tame. I bet this pony can really jump. Try her on the four footers in the outdoor field."

Did Jasper really mean four foot jumps? Jess tingled nervously.

"Hang on a minute." Amy's voice was steady but concerned. "Jess has only just got this pony, Jasper. She's not really familiar with her. Besides, Skylark's probably tired with everything that's happened today. She really needs rest. And the ground outside is very hard still..."

Jess heard Amy's words and knew she was right,

but now Jasper was talking again. "Nonsense, she'll be fine," he said. "And if Jess is willing, then I say let her jump. I'm sure she can get the pony round the course."

Jess looked from one face to the other.

"We could just try one," she volunteered, anxious to please.

Amy gave a deep sigh. "Don't feel you have to do everything today Jess. It's exciting having a new pony, but she'll still be here tomorrow."

"Come on," Jasper said. "Follow me to the outdoor school."

Quickly, Jasper led the way out of the covered arena and into a white fenced enclosure. A course of ten huge jumps stood in the afternoon light. Skylark shifted and danced on the spot. Jess looked at Amy's quietly troubled face. I can't back out now, Jess thought to herself.

"Come on Jess, you don't need to do the whole course. Just take her over the parallel bars and the brush. Let's see what this little beauty can do," Jasper was calling now.

Jess turned Skylark determinedly towards the first parallel and shortened the reins. Skylark's step was light and quick as Jess leaned forward in the saddle and urged her on. Now they were approaching the first parallel, steady, not too fast. Skylark's hooves thudded over the hard ground and Jess counted her point of take-off. One, two, three and they were soaring through the air, then they had landed again. Then it was on to the next parallel. They sailed over that with inches to spare and Jess couldn't help grinning madly. Jasper was right – Skylark was a superb jumper. What's more, she really seemed to be enjoying herself, flicking her tail playfully and giving little dancing, kicking steps. Jess was enjoying herself too. The feeling was marvellous. Now they only had the brush left. Jess turned Skylark swiftly and they pounded towards it. Within seconds they were suspended in mid-air and Jess's spirits soared with delight.

After that everything seemed to happen in slow-motion. Skylark's forelegs met the ground and hit a patch of frozen ground directly at landing point. There was nothing to grip on to and her legs splayed out in front of her while her hind legs followed. Jess didn't know much after that – just that she was thrown to the ground and Skylark lay a little way ahead of her, lifeless where she had fallen.

"No..." someone was screaming. As Jess scrambled to her feet she realized the voice was her own.

"Oh no!" Amy cried simultaneously and both girls rushed over to where the horse lay. As Jess drew nearer she saw that Skylark's flanks were heaving and she was panting heavily. Suddenly, with a supreme effort, the little grey pony raised her head and stumbled her way up to a standing position.

"Skylark," Jess cried.

"Stand back." Jasper's voice was stern, but he looked worried. "She just seems a bit winded that's all," he said briefly. "Probably knocked her knees. Amy, bring her back to her stable and get her untacked."

"No... I want to do it!" Jess cried in anguish.

Jasper put his hands up in surprise. "Fair enough," he said. "Amy, call the vet, just to be on the safe side. I want this pony seen quickly. Her picture and

Rychester will be all over the *Daily Advertiser* tomorrow. We can't let anything happen to her." And with that, he marched off.

Jess was only dimly aware of this conversation, she was so worried about Skylark. She could kick herself for having been so stupid.

"She will be all right, won't she?" Jess asked Amy fearfully.

"She'll be fine." Amy's voice was soothing. "Come on, let's get Skylark to her stable."

8

THINGS GET BETTER

"She'll need total rest for three days. It's just a nasty knock to the knees," the vet said, smiling kindly. She snapped her bag shut and walked back to her car, green boots crunching along the gravel on the ground.

Jess watched her go and then turned back to Skylark's stable. Once inside, she flung her arms around the little pony's neck and buried her face into the soft mane.

"Everything's going to be all right, Skylark," she said.

Jess felt inconsolable. She shouldn't have jumped Skylark straight away. It was a miracle that she was all right.

"Is everything OK?" A voice roused Jess from her thoughts and she turned to see Camilla regarding her from the yard. Jess groaned inwardly. The last thing she needed at that moment was any of Camilla's advice. But strangely, Camilla was being nice. "I heard about the accident," she continued. "It was bad luck. Daddy said you and Skylark were jumping well."

The words 'jumping well' registered immediately with Jess and were enough to ignite a small flicker of pride, but it was what Camilla said first that she didn't understand.

"Daddy?" She repeated the words slowly.

"Yes," Camilla said. "He was watching you."

"But only Amy and Jasper were there," Jess said in confusion. Had someone else been watching her jump as well?

"Jess, are you being deliberately dense?" Camilla shook her head. "Jasper *is* my father. I'm Camilla Carlisle. Didn't anyone tell you that? Surely Amy must have mentioned it."

"No," Jess said slowly. "No, she didn't."

"Well that was very slack of her. Anyway, I'm just about to take Apollo out for a ride. There's some really good galloping along the coast. Why don't you come with me?"

"But – Skylark," Jess indicated her pony. "The vet said she must rest for at least three days."

Camilla gave an impatient toss of her head. "Honestly Jess, there's nothing really wrong with her."

"The vet said she had to rest. I'm not going to risk it." Jess was quiet but firm.

Camilla pursed her lips and raised her eyebrows. "Well if you feel like that," she said at last. "Then I'll get Amy to tack up Dido instead. She's not being ridden at the moment."

"Well, I don't know, I sort of thought I would stay and look after Skylark," Jess said.

"Oh come on, Jess," Camilla said. "Don't be so wet. It'll be fun. Skylark will be fine here. Amy'll keep an eye on her."

Jess looked from Skylark to Camilla. She was furious that Camilla had called her wet. She would show her. Besides, it was a marvellous day for a ride.

"All right," she said finally. "But *I'll* tack up Dido."

Camilla shrugged. "Amy's supposed to do that kind of stuff. It's what she's paid for."

"It's what I'm used to," Jess said firmly.

"Suit yourself," Camilla said as she headed off to find Apollo.

Jess turned to Skylark again. "I'll be back soon," she promised, checking the pony's haynet was full. "You take it easy here. It won't be long before we're riding together again."

Mounted on Dido, Jess met up with Camilla in the yard. "All ready?" Camilla called over her shoulder. "Let's go."

She walked Apollo a little way in front of Jess and Dido as they made their way out of the stables and along the country lanes that wound away from Rychester.

Behind her, Jess tried to adjust herself to Dido's rhythm, and settle into the saddle. She was nervous about riding a new pony, especially one as impressive as Dido. Her apprehension wasn't helped when she saw the nonchalant way Camilla rode Apollo. Jess could see that the palomino was skittish. She pirouetted and skipped along the road, spooking at every moving twig. But Camilla didn't seem bothered at all. She controlled the nervous pony with off-hand grace, even turning around to chat to Jess about

48

nothing in particular. Her apparent ease helped to calm Jess, and soon she began to enjoy Dido's regular pace. As they turned the ponies into a field, Jess brought Dido level with Apollo.

"We're heading towards my stables," she told Camilla. "I mean, the stables I used to ride at – Sandy Lane."

"Never heard of it," Camilla shrugged.

"Well it's a lot smaller than Rychester," Jess said. "But it's a lovely place."

"I'll take your word for it," Camilla said. "Of course nowhere could be as great as Rychester. It was my love of horses that inspired Daddy to set it up. He's a business man really, but he adores animals and with the profits from his cosmetics company he started Rychester. Now he's got a stable full of winning horses!"

"There are some lovely horses at Rychester," Jess agreed with a slight pang of envy. Fancy having a dad who was willing to set up a riding stables just because his daughter loved horses.

"We only have the best, Jess." Camilla flashed a wide grin. "And now we've got Skylark too. She's going to do really well for Rychester, you just see if she doesn't. Come on, let's gallop!"

And with that Camilla turned Apollo to the open grass and spurred him on with her heels. In the next moment they had raced the length of the field. Jess was so astonished at this abrupt departure that she wasn't able to check Dido, who danced excitedly beneath her and then was off, charging after Apollo like a streak of lightning. Jess didn't have time to think, and in the next moment she had settled into the gallop with elation, the wind whistling through her hair. As Dido came to a halt beside Apollo, Camilla grinned at Jess.

"That was brilliant, wasn't it?" she cried. "Bet I surprised you."

Jess, catching her breath, could only smile back and nod.

The first thing Jess did after the ride was over and she had untacked and stabled Dido, was to run around and check on Skylark. As she drew nearer to the pony's box she saw Jasper leaning against the door. Jess's heart sank. Had something happened to Skylark? Then she saw that he was talking to someone, and that the someone was Penny Webster from the *Daily Advertiser*. What was she doing back so soon? Skylark stood looking out over her stable door.

"Is everything all right?" Jess asked anxiously, nodding at Skylark.

"Absolutely," Jasper replied quickly. "Penny and I were just sorting out a bit more publicity for you and this pony here. Just a few informal pictures, that's all."

"Along with the rest of the team." Penny smiled.

"Team? What team?" Jess was puzzled. What was Penny talking about?

"Look, I'll ring you in the week, Jasper." Penny turned to go. "Oh, look out for Tuesday's *Daily Advertiser*," she said to Jess as she went. "The picture of you and Skylark will be on the second page." And then she was gone.

Jasper turned to Jess. "Look Jess," he said. "I didn't tell Penny about Skylark's little accident. Didn't see much point really. After all, the vet said she'd be better in a day or two. Anyway there's something more important I want to discuss with you."

Jess wondered fleetingly what could be more important than Skylark's health. But now Jasper was talking again and what he said made her gasp.

"That team Penny mentioned," Jasper explained. "It's for the Ash Hill show. I'm relying on you and Skylark to do well in the open-jumping. If you do, your score would count towards a team medal for Rychester. We need five riders. Camilla will be entering too, and then there'll be another three Rychester riders."

"The Ash Hill show?" Jess echoed slowly, her heart beginning to beat faster with excitement. "But do you think I'll be ready, Jasper? I've hardly ridden Skylark at all yet. I wanted to take things slowly. Get to know her first."

"That's very admirable, Jess," Jasper said. "But I think you're being rather overcautious. You and Skylark will be fine. I've seen you ride. Ash Hill's a month and a half away after all, and Skylark has had excellent training. She should do well for us. And so will you – with some Rychester tuition."

"But I can't afford lessons–"

"Don't worry," Jasper said, holding his hand up in the air. "I'll take care of all that. But don't forget that I pay for the best and I expect the best from Rychester teachers and pupils alike."

And that it seemed was that. As Jasper walked away, Jess was left reeling with excitement and shock. She turned to Skylark.

"Everything's happening so quickly, Skylark," she whispered into the pony's ear. "Not so long ago I didn't even have a pony and I had to muck out in return for my rides. Now I've got a pony of my own, I'm part of this smart stables *and* I'm going to jump at Ash Hill too."

Skylark turned away and began pulling at her haynet. As Jess slid back the bolt on the door, she was interrupted again by Camilla's voice. This time she was calling to her from across the stable yard.

"Jess, would you like to come and have some tea at my house? I want to show you something."

Jess thought hard. She ought to go, especially if they were to be part of a team together. Jess gave Skylark a final check and, deciding the pony was all right, hurried out of the stable to follow Camilla.

"Come on," Camilla said, leading Jess to the grand, gabled house she'd seen the day she'd first visited Rychester. So this was where Camilla lived. It was a far cry from her own, rather shabby cottage. As she walked through the front door of Camilla's house. Jess looked around in awe at the cool marbled entrance hall.

"Is that you Camilla darling?" A shrill voice echoed into the hallway and soon a taller version of Camilla, dressed in smart pale trousers and a long jacket, emerged in the hallway.

"Hi Mum, we're starving," Camilla announced loudly.

"Oh, are you?" Camilla's mother seemed perplexed. "I'm just off out, darling. You'll have to forage in the kitchen I'm afraid."

"OK," Camilla replied. "This is Jess by the way. She won the pony – you know, Dad's competition."

"How lovely," Camilla's mother smiled with brief distraction at Jess, who smiled shyly back. "See you later darlings," she said, and with that she was gone.

"Come on," Camilla said to Jess.

She led the way into a vast kitchen. Stainless steel cupboards lined the walls, spotless and gleaming. Camilla delved into one of them and drew out a tin. "Chocolate digestives," she announced triumphantly. "We'll take these up to my room."

Camilla marched up the stairs and down a long corridor, past several closed doors. Finally she stopped outside one of them.

"Here we are," she said, turning the handle and Jess followed her in.

Camilla's room was decorated in pink. The walls were painted with hundreds of tiny stars and a four poster bed was swathed in pink muslin in the middle of the room. Pink and white curtains draped the windows and the floor was covered with a thick pink carpet. Shelves around the room were lined with bottles of creams and lotions, all with the distinctive green Vrai Vert logo.

"I've got hundreds of bottles of the stuff," Camilla laughed, seeing Jess looking at the bottles. "Here, take some home." And before Jess could protest, Camilla had thrust a wicker basket of Vrai Vert goodies into her hands.

"Um, thanks," Jess mumbled and then thought that perhaps she should have sounded more grateful. After all, her mother would be pleased.

"What do you think?" Camilla said, indicating the room.

"It must have cost a fortune," Jess said, impressed. "Is pink your favourite colour?"

"What? Oh, not especially," Camilla replied in an off-hand way. "Mummy chose it all and then had it photographed by some design magazine."

This all sounded rather glamorous to Jess, but Camilla didn't seem impressed. "This is all boring," Camilla said. "Come and look at these."

Camilla darted across the room to a small alcove, stepping carelessly on a discarded sweater on the way. Inside the alcove was a glass cabinet and inside that were cups, trophies and rosettes, all lined up on display. *Camilla Carlisle, First, New Benningdon Horse Trials*, one trophy inscription read. *Dressage First Place, Southdown Show*, read another. *First Prize, Colcott Cross Country Team Chase,* another was engraved.

"Wow." Jess was suitably impressed as she inspected the gleaming trophies.

"The Ash Hill Team Event will soon be joining them," Camilla announced. "You're very lucky – not many girls would be able to join the team just like that, you know. These are only some of the trophies," Camilla went on. "Daddy's got the main ones displayed downstairs."

"Did you win all these with Apollo?" Jess asked, picturing Camilla and her beautiful palomino pony jumping effortlessly clear at show after show.

"Some of them," Camilla said. "But I've won on other horses too. Daddy's horses, Jess. That's why I'm showing you these. Daddy only has the best horses and now we've got Skylark. She's going to win loads of prizes for Rychester, Jess. She's a very special pony."

"I know she's special," Jess said. "But remember she is my pony, Camilla, not Rychester's."

"Of course she is, silly." Camilla flashed her a quick smile, and after the briefest of pauses spoke again. "Look Jess," she said. "I hope you don't think me rude, but those jods you're wearing must have seen better days."

Jess felt embarrassed as she looked down at her scruffy, old jodphurs. She couldn't even remember how long she'd had them.

"I'm sure you'll be getting some new clothes, but I'm only mentioning it because Mummy's just bought me two new pairs of jods," Camilla continued lightly. "Would you like my old ones?"

She fished around in the bottom of a wardrobe and produced what to Jess looked like a brand new pair of beige jodhpurs.

"They're just about your size I think," Camilla said now. "Take them. I was only going to throw them out."

"Well, if you're sure..." Jess was hesitant but she wasn't proud either. It was obvious that Camilla's parents could well afford to buy her new clothes and that Camilla would have no hesitation in discarding anything she'd lost interest in. Jess accepted the jodhpurs graciously and Camilla smiled broadly.

"You can wear them when you ride Skylark again," she said. "It won't be long now. And then we'll really have fun. We're going to have some brilliant hacks together. Just see if we don't."

Her enthusiasm made Jess grin excitedly. "We will have fun," she said to herself. "And I've got my very own pony to ride. Brilliant!"

9

JESS MOVES ON

Jess sat at the kitchen table, chatting to her mother who was making supper. From time to time a strand of hair would fall over her mother's face and she would push it back wearily with a damp hand. Jess thought her mum looked tired and dowdy in her ancient leggings and baggy old sweater.

For what must have been the fifteenth time that day, Jess began to talk about Rychester again.

"Mrs. Carlisle had Camilla's room photographed for a magazine," she said. "And Camilla's dad set up Rychester Riding Stables just for Camilla. Isn't that amazing?"

"Fascinating Jess," her mother said brightly. "I'll have to see what I can do to make your life just that little bit more glamorous. Now, what can I do for your supper tonight? I know you won't want spaghetti bolognese like the rest of us, will you?"

"Not really Mum, sorry," Jess said, guiltily. She knew that not eating meat caused her mother extra work. But no matter how many times she said she'd just have the vegetables, or make herself a sandwich while the rest of her family tucked into chicken or bacon, her mother would always go out of her way to make her something else.

"You're a growing girl, Jess," she would say. "You can't survive on sandwiches. I'll just have to cook you something different."

Guiltily, Jess turned away and let her thoughts go back to Rychester. She had spent every evening that week at the stables, and she couldn't help talking about it. Skylark and she were getting better and better and the more time she spent at Rychester, the more she liked it. Amy was encouraging and Camilla had really taken her under her wing. And Skylark – well, Skylark was the most wonderful pony in the world, and her very own too.

Of course, Jess still wished that the accident hadn't happened, but Skylark was better now. Jasper had been right, there was no point in telling people what had gone on. Certainly it would only worry Jess's mum and dad.

Most of all, Jess didn't want to tell Rosie about it. It was embarrassment and pride that stopped her. Rosie had already voiced her doubts about Rychester and Jess had decided that there was no point in fuelling them. Indeed, she had tried to avoid talking about Skylark to Rosie. Guiltily she realized she'd hardly spoken to her all week. They had both been busy, so it had been rather difficult. Rosie was involved in netball trials after school, and Jess had been at Rychester for the past few evenings. So when the phone rang a few moments later, Jess was pleased to hear Rosie's voice at the other end.

"I just wondered if you were around at the weekend," Rosie said. "There's a beach ride going out from Sandy Lane. Do you want to bring Skylark along?"

"Um–" Jess hesitated, not knowing what to say. It would be a week after Skylark's accident. Several days after the vet had said she'd be OK to ride, but Jess didn't want to push the pony and she had been planning to ride her quietly in the indoor school, under Amy's supervision.

"I don't think I can, Rosie," she said. "You see, I'm not really used to Skylark yet," she tried. "I think I should get to know her a bit first before I take her out on a hack."

"Fair enough." Rosie's voice was quiet but understanding at the end of the line. "I saw another picture of you in the paper by the way. Lovely cheesy grin!"

"What, me or Skylark?" Jess laughed now.

"You of course," Rosie chortled. "Skylark looks beautiful. In black and white anyway."

"She is beautiful, Rosie," Jess said quickly now. "And you will see her soon, I promise."

"I can't wait," Rosie replied eagerly. "I was beginning to think you'd forgotten all about your old Sandy Lane mates. Are you a Rychester girl now? Posh clothes, daring riding style, that kind of thing?"

"Oh Rychester's not so bad," Jess said quickly. "In fact, it's better than I expected... you should see it

58

Rosie." Jess's voice rose with excitement. "The loose boxes are huge, and really smart. That girl we saw on the cliff top ride, the one with the palomino pony, remember? Well, she's Camilla Carlisle, the daughter of Rychester's owner, Jasper... she seemed really snooty at first, but she's all right underneath it all. And the horses at Rychester are wonderful. There's Apollo, and Dido and Skylark of course–" Jess paused for breath. "And I'm riding at Ash Hill too, for Rychester. Jasper Carlisle and everyone at Rychester reckon Skylark's going to be brilliant at jumping. She's really responsive to ride."

"Well it all sounds perfect," Rosie said brightly. Suddenly Jess realized that she hadn't asked Rosie about Sandy Lane at all. How could she have been so selfish?

"What's the news at Sandy Lane?" she asked quickly, twisting the telephone cord around her fingers. "Am I missing anything?"

"Not really," Rosie said. "Nick's been in a bad mood because his flu's come back and lots of people seem to be cancelling rides. I'm definitely jumping Pepper at the Ash Hill Show in the Open Jumping."

As Rosie chattered on, Jess's mind drifted back to Skylark. She couldn't wait to ride her pony again. She wondered what Skylark was doing now. Was she was all right? Had Amy checked her for the night? Suddenly Jess realized that Rosie was asking her something.

"Jess," Rosie called, "Jess are you there?"

"Yes," Jess said quickly. And then because Rosie's hurt silence hung in the air, Jess added. "It sounds like things are pretty busy then."

"I guess so." Rosie's voice was quiet and Jess felt wretched and embarrassed for not paying her more attention. "I have to go," she lied miserably. "My mum's calling me for supper."

10

OLD FRIENDS NEW FRIENDS

It was a Saturday afternoon. Jess adjusted Skylark's saddle and did up the girth.

"Are you ready for a hack, Skylark?" she whispered into the pony's ear. "Because I am."

The last two weeks had been busy. There was school and homework and after school jobs around the house to fit in as well. Every evening, as soon as she was able, Jess would cycle the twenty minutes to Rychester to spend time with Skylark. At the end of the first week, she had ridden her pony at last.

"You've been wise to wait," Amy told her encouragingly as she had watched Jess ride in the warmth of the indoor school. Skylark had been perfectly sound and to Jess's delight, there seemed to be no lasting damage to the pony's knees. One evening there was another publicity photo session with the *Daily Advertiser*, the Rychester Stables sign prominently displayed in the background.

"Let's show them a fit and eager pony, and a healthy and happy rider," Jasper had urged Jess, shoving a bottle of *New Improved Mango Miracle Shampoo* into her hand as she smiled broadly for the camera.

Camilla was often at the stables in the evening too. She would ride Apollo in the indoor school, training him for the Ash Hill show, and Jess watched them jump with admiration. Apollo cleared the jumps effortlessly, with a proud flick of his tail. Jess noticed that Camilla kept him on a very tight rein which caused the palomino pony to skip and toss his head. But the more Apollo pirouetted, the tighter Camilla sat to the saddle. She didn't flinch or move a muscle.

After all the lessons in the indoor school during the week, Jess was looking forward to a relaxing hack in the open air. She swung herself up into Skylark's saddle and gathered up the reins. Just as she was preparing to walk on, a voice at her shoulder stopped her.

"Give Skylark a good run now." Jasper's voice was brisk and efficient. "She needs the exercise."

"Yes," Jess replied eagerly, "But I'm not going to take any risks."

"Absolutely," Jasper said. "You need to save yourself and that pony for the Ash Hill Show. After all it's not only Rychester you'll be jumping for. The *Daily Advertiser* will be following your progress with interest too. So you'd better come back with a rosette. Now go on, enjoy the hack."

He gave Skylark a smart slap on the rump and the little pony lurched forward. Jess, temporarily unseated, put a steadying hand on the front of the saddle and thought about what Jasper had said... 'you'd better come back with a rosette'. Jess felt vaguely uneasy, bullied almost. But Jasper was relying on her and that made her feel important.

"We'll have to train really hard Skylark," she whispered to her pony. "But we can do it."

"We can do it," she repeated silently to herself and her heart began to beat faster as she thought about the competition. She was a part of this place now, and she would do well for Rychester. She couldn't wait to talk more about Ash Hill with Camilla, and as she walked on towards where Camilla and Apollo were waiting, a thought occurred to her.

"Camilla, do you want to do some training for Rychester tonight?" she asked her new friend as she drew nearer. "Apollo's quite fearless around the ring, it might be good for Skylark to follow him and see what kind of a team we'd really make."

Camilla glanced at her impatiently. "Tonight? Sorry, Jess, I'm busy. Lucy and Samantha are coming round for supper. Now come on, slow coach, we've been waiting ages for you. Let's get going!"

Jess felt strangely deflated that she hadn't been included in Camilla's plans as she followed on out of the stables and down the lane. Still, she couldn't think about that now. The ride was winding its way out of the yard.

Samantha rode her brown pony, Amber, Lucy was on Dido, and Allison was riding Rychester's Jackdaw. These were the same girls who had ridden with Camilla that day on the cliff tops. But like Camilla, they had shown no sign of having recognized Jess.

Well, why should they? Jess thought. I look

completely different. Now I'm riding a beautifully turned-out pony and wearing Camilla's smart jods and I've even brushed my hair.

Jess had taken to washing her hair with Camilla's shampoo which really did make it smell nice.

I look completely different from when I was riding shaggy little Minstrel in my scruffy old anorak, Jess thought to herself.

"So you're jumping Skylark at Ash Hill?" Samantha interrupted her thoughts as the ride clattered down the lane.

"Yes." Jess threw her reply back over her shoulder. "If we're ready."

"You'll be ready," Camilla joined in. "Anyway, Apollo's bound to win tons of stuff. You can watch me and see how it's done, Jess."

"Honestly, Camilla," Allison retorted. "You're such a show-off. All five of us are entered for Ash Hill. And there's a good chance we might win the team medal if our scores are any good."

Camilla smiled gleefully. "That's true, Allison, so of course you might win something," she conceded. "But it'll be me and Apollo galloping away with the Open Jumping trophy."

"Show us how you're going to do it then, Cam." Allison's voice was excited as they turned the ponies off the lane and into a stubble field. "See those logs over there?"

She pointed to the edge of the field where a pile of timber was stacked toweringly high. Sharp twigs and coarse brush stuck out from the log pile, and the whole construction looked very precarious. "Bet you can't jump that."

Camilla followed her gaze and laughed scornfully. "What, that tame old pile of wood?" she crowed. "Child's play. But if I do it, you lot will be too chicken to follow me."

"Brilliant, a dare!" Allison cried. "I'm right behind you, Camilla."

"Me too!" said Lucy.

"Count me in then," Samantha added.

"What about you, Jess?" Camilla turned Apollo to face Skylark. "Fancy a challenge?"

Jess looked at the precarious pile of wood. It was very high. One knock from a pony's hoof and the whole lot would come crashing dangerously down. There was another problem too. The point of take-off for the jump was clear enough, but the timber was placed at the edge of the woods. The landing point wasn't visible. It would be like jumping blind. It was crazy... mad. Skylark pulled at the reins and sniffed the wind impatiently. Jess shifted uncomfortably in the saddle. They were all looking at her.

"Scared?" Allison sneered.

"It's just stupid," Jess said fiercely. "A stupid thing to do."

" Yep, she's scared," Allison cried triumphantly.

"No she's not," Camilla said, looking directly at Jess. "She'll follow us. Won't you Jess?" And before Jess could say anything, Camilla turned Apollo sharply and kicked him into a gallop across the field.

Jess could hardly watch as they approached the timber pile at break-neck speed. Surely they would crash straight into it. At the very last moment, Camilla must have checked Apollo because he seemed to stop still in mid-gallop. And then, like a harrier jump-jet taking off, he sprang over the logs with inches to spare. On landing, Camilla pulled him up sharply to avoid the trees and the horse turned on the spot before stopping directly at the edge of the forest. Camilla gave a wave and beckoned the rest of the ride to follow.

"Come on Jess, live a little," Samantha called over her shoulder as she urged Amber on to meet the jump.

Jess took a deep breath as she watched them all go. Now Samantha was clear, and Lucy too. Skylark pulled and pulled at the reins, pawing at the ground as she walked in impatient circles. The air was crisp and clear and suddenly Jess felt a surge of confidence. Skylark was just as good as any of those ponies... better even. Suddenly the jump looked exciting and inviting.

As Allison pushed Jackdaw safely over the timber, Jess's mind was made up. Skylark didn't need to be told a second time to gallop, and in an instant the little grey pony was flying across the ground. Jess's spirits soared with every step the pony took.

And now the timber pile loomed nearer, even larger than Jess had anticipated. Keeping a firm but light hold of the reins she focused straight ahead, right between Skylark's alert ears. She could just make out the rest of the ride, waiting for her on the other side of the jump. As she drew near to her point of take-off, they seemed to multiply. Suddenly it looked as if there were lots of ponies and riders. Jess screwed up her eyes to see better. But suddenly here was the jump, and with a swift kick she urged Skylark on. Now they were soaring lightly through the air. When they landed – a little shakily, but clear – Jess's momentary feeling of elation gave way to blind panic as she saw she was hurtling straight for a group of horses who had emerged from the woods a little way beyond the jump.

"Look out!" a familiar voice cried.

At the last minute, Jess gave an almighty tug on Skylark's reins and swung the surprised pony around to the left, away from the crowd – just in time to avoid a collision.

"Jess!" the same familiar voice said. "What on earth do you think you're playing at? You could have killed someone."

Tom Buchanan sat looking down at her from Chancey. He shook his head slowly.

"Tom!" Jess gasped. Of course, it was the 2 o'clock Sandy Lane hack.

"You obviously didn't see us riding out of the woods," Tom continued, and his voice was tight with anger. "This pile of timber is right by the trees. If we'd been a fraction later riding out and hadn't seen you careering towards us, there could have been a really nasty accident."

"I–" Jess began, but she was lost for words. It was Camilla who jumped to her rescue.

"Oh shut up Grandad," she sneered at Tom. "This is a fantastic jump and Jess cleared it beautifully."

Samantha, Lucy and Allison laughed heartily but Jess reddened at Camilla's words. Tom went puce with rage and shot Jess a filthy look, but he said nothing. Jess squirmed with embarrassment and stared at the ground. She so desperately wanted to apologize, but that look had said it all. Tom was disgusted with her and Jess was mortified. Tom had always been such a good friend, but now he turned Chancey away in silent fury and rode on without a backward glance.

Then suddenly there was Rosie riding towards her,

on the back of dear old Pepper. At once Jess felt a pang of sadness.

Rosie trotted Pepper to a halt alongside Skylark and whispered across to Jess.

"Don't think much of your new friends, Jess, but you did clear that jump spectacularly. I'd never have had the nerve. So this is Skylark?" she went on. "She's beautiful."

Suddenly Jess missed Sandy Lane very much. Most of all she missed all the fun she'd had with Rosie.

"Why don't I bring Skylark over to Sandy Lane this evening, Rosie?" she suggested eagerly. "You could ride her then."

"Oh that's a lovely idea, Jess," Rosie shrugged apologetically. "But I'm going to the cinema with Izzy tonight."

Jess gave a small smile and tried to sound cheerful. She knew she shouldn't, but she couldn't help feeling a tiny bit jealous. Swiftly she thrust the thought to the back of her mind. "Well, maybe another time," she said.

"I'd like that," Rosie said, as she followed the Sandy Lane ride out of the woods.

Jess watched her go, until Camilla's strident voice rang in her ears. "Come on Jess," she urged. "Let's leave these geriatrics to it."

"See you soon, Rosie," Jess called hopefully after her departing friend, and with a sigh she turned Skylark into the woods.

At the end of the hour, the Rychester ride wound its way back to the stables. They'd had several good gallops and jumped some small logs, but they were still full of the success of clearing the timber pile and chattered eagerly to one another.

"Just wait till we get to Ash Hill," Camilla cried. "We'll be the best showjumpers they've ever seen."

Only Jess remained silent for most of the time.

When they reached the yard, Jess swung down from Skylark's saddle and led her towards the loose boxes. Ahead, she could see Amy with her back to her, talking urgently to someone Jess couldn't make out.

"I couldn't really say," Amy was shaking her head at the person she was talking to. "It's just what my cousin Barry tells me really."

"Well, let me know if you hear anything else," a voice was saying. "Keep an eye on Jasper perhaps."

But before Jess had time to wonder what they were talking about, Amy had shifted position and Jess saw it was Penny Webster from the *Daily Advertiser*. At the same time Penny caught sight of Jess too.

"Jess, there you are," she said. "I was just asking Amy where I might find you."

"Oh." Jess was hesitant. Surely Penny wasn't here to organize more publicity photos.

"I came by to find out how you were getting on with Skylark," Penny said. "Are you pleased with your prize pony?"

"Oh yes." Jess's hesitance gave way to eager enthusiasm. "She's just brilliant. Thanks."

"Well she looks lovely," Penny said, walking towards them and giving Skylark a pat.

"Do you want me to untack and groom her?" Amy asked.

"No of course not." Jess shook her head. "I want to do it myself, but thanks anyway, Amy."

"Good for you." Amy smiled. "I don't suppose

Camilla will be so keen. I'd better go and find out what state she's left poor Apollo in. See you later."

"I'll be in touch," Penny called to Amy before turning back to Jess. "Well, I'm glad you're all right. I'd better be going. See you soon, Jess," she smiled. And with a quick wave she was gone.

"Hmm, that was a flying visit," Jess said to Skylark as she led the pony to her stable. "Come on now, let's get this saddle off."

11

THE COMPETITION LOOMS

"So how's this pony of yours, Jess? Fed up with it yet?" Jess's father pushed the log around the fire-grate and watched as it caught flames. A warm cosy glow filled the small sitting room.

"Don't be silly, Dad," Jess laughed as she stood by the door, pulling her boots on. "I'll never get fed up of Skylark."

"Well, I must say, you seem to have got it all worked out. You've organized everything very well, with the stabling and taking care of the pony, and keeping up your school work too. I admire your dedication."

Jess smiled. For a fleeting moment she was tempted to join him by the fireside and read her new pony book. But only for a moment, for Skylark was waiting for her and there was Ash Hill to practise for. She waved goodbye to her dad and braced herself against the March wind as she battled her bicycle down the garden path.

Ash Hill was now only three weeks away, but Jess had been training hard. Jasper was very excited and had hired Martin Jennings, ex-Olympic riding star, to train the Ash Hill entrants, all at his own expense. "He'll get you jumping like winners," Jasper had announced.

The jumping lessons were gruelling, and the jumps they had to tackle, high. But Jess was jumping well and Martin Jennings seemed pleased with her progress.

On this Saturday morning, Jasper stood in the middle of the jumping ring next to Martin and watched as Jess set off to the first. Lucy, on Dido, had just knocked two fences down, but Jess, concentrating hard, thundered clear around the course. She should have been elated, but Jasper's presence was putting a damper on things. When she brought Skylark back to a walk, Jasper called to Jess.

"That was far too hesitant," he said. "Push her straight at the jump. You've got to show her who's boss."

Jess swallowed hard and patted Skylark, despite Jasper's harsh words.

Next it was Allison's turn for Jasper's advice as she pushed Jackdaw cautiously over the obstacles. They were going well, but this wasn't good enough for Jasper. "Too slow, Allison!" he cried. "You'll lose us vital marks if you don't step up the pace."

Allison went red and trotted Jackdaw to the far side of the ring. Samantha was next to jump on Amber. They did all right until the final wall, which Amber just caught with her rear hoof. The top brick came crashing down and Samantha rode her pony out of the ring, shaking her head.

Jasper's reaction was immediate and unforgiving.

"You lost concentration, Samantha!" he shouted. "You thought Amber was home and dry. You relaxed and it cost you four faults. That's four faults I don't want to see at Ash Hill. Understood?"

Samantha hung her head and mumbled a "yes".

Jess winced inwardly and gave her a sympathetic glance. Samantha had jumped a good round. One fence down wasn't exactly a disaster. But Jasper was a hard taskmaster, as well as interfering. Jess could see it was difficult for Martin Jennings to teach them with Jasper breathing down his neck. Still, Martin was an excellent teacher and all the Ash Hill entrants had really improved. It was obvious that Jasper expected nothing less than a first for Rychester at Ash Hill, and with Martin's tuition, it was clear they were in with a real chance.

Still, Jess shivered in her saddle. Jasper demanded perfection from his riders. But perfection wasn't always realistic, Nick had told her that enough times.

Jess considered these thoughts silently as she watched Camilla spur Apollo over the first combination. Apollo cleared the jumps spectacularly and swiftly.

"Wow, that was a brilliant round, Camilla," Jess called over as Camilla rode clear out of the jumping ring.

"Well done, Camilla," Martin smiled quickly.

"Much better," Jasper roared. But even this late praise couldn't raise Jess's spirits. Jess was glad when at last the lesson was over and, in low spirits, she jumped to the ground and ran the stirrups up.

"You jumped very well, Skylark," she whispered as she led the pony back to her stable.

She slipped the bridle off Skylark's nose and hung it on the stable door. Skylark lifted her head to her haynet and began to chomp. As Jess lifted the heavy saddle down from her back and made her way with it to the tack room, she whistled softly to herself. She didn't think she could ever get bored with this familiar routine of untacking and settling her pony – her very own pony! She thought of all the other ponies she had looked after – Minstrel and Pepper and Hector and Storm Cloud. Jess paused. Storm Cloud! Before the pony had gone lame, Jess's greatest pleasure had been riding the delicate grey Arab. Since Skylark, Jess had hardly given Storm Cloud another thought.

"Is that what happens when you have your own pony?" Jess said to herself. "Poor Stormy, I wonder if her leg's any better. Maybe I should ride over to Sandy Lane this afternoon and see her. I should at least see if Rosie wants to ride Skylark after all this time."

She paused, considering all this, and thought of Skylark, content in her stable.

"I'll ride there now," she determined. "Before Skylark gets too settled. She's still fresh enough."

She had almost reached the tack room and was about to turn back to Skylark's stable when she heard shouting and angry voices coming from inside the tack room. Jess hesitated. She didn't want to eavesdrop, but she couldn't help hearing snatches of conversation. The voices were so loud it was hard not to. It was definitely Jasper in there, his enraged tones were all too familiar. The other voice sounded like Amy's. But it was an Amy that Jess hardly recognized. This Amy

74

was shouting angrily. Jess was stunned. Amy was usually so calm and restrained. Perhaps Jasper was really telling her off.

Jess dithered. Maybe she should go into the tack room and pretend she hadn't heard what was going on, then Jasper would have to stop his telling-off and Amy would be all right. Jess glanced nervously around the stable yard. There was no one else in sight. From inside the tack room the argument raged.

"What did you say to the press about me?" Jasper screamed.

"Nothing," Amy spat back. "Why? Do you have something to hide Jasper?"

Zoom! A huge jet roared over head and Amy's voice was drowned out. Jess turned on her heel and rushed back to Skylark's stable.

"Well, it's a good job we're going out on another ride after all, girl," she said to the surprised pony. "Trying to put your saddle back in its proper place would have been like walking into a lion's den. Come on, let's go and see some old friends of mine."

****

Half an hour later, Jess and Skylark turned into Sandy Lane. Jess's heart pounded as she neared the stable buildings. Everything seemed very quiet as she slipped down from the saddle and led Skylark along the row of stables, looking for Storm Cloud.

Suddenly Jess's heart leapt. There was dear Stormy now, poking her delicate grey nose out of the last stable door. But Jess hesitated, for Storm Cloud was not alone. Hunched over the door a familiar figure stood talking softly to the pony. Jess stopped silently as she observed Nick Brooks checking on his horses.

Suddenly Skylark snorted and shuffled her hooves noisily on the stone path. Storm Cloud whinnied in reply and Nick turned his head sharply. He saw Jess at once.

"Hello," he said. "We haven't seen you around here for a while. Everyone's out on a hack I'm afraid."

"Oh." Jess was almost embarrassed as she tried to explain. "What with one thing and another, I realized I'd almost forgotten about poor old Stormy," she began.

"Well, she certainly hasn't forgotten you," Nick laughed as Storm Cloud craned her head over the stable door and chewed expectantly at Jess's coat pocket.

"Looking for treats I presume?" Nick smiled.

"Well she's in luck," said Jess triumphantly, fishing out a stray sugar lump from the depths of her pocket. "I saved one just for her."

"Better not make this other one jealous," Nick said, indicating Skylark. "Is this your prize pony?"

"Um, yes." Jess's pride in Skylark was tinged with shame at not bringing her to see Nick sooner.

"She's lovely," Nick smiled kindly and rubbed Skylark's nose. "And how's Rychester working out?"

"Oh." Jess didn't know what to say. She thought of Jasper Carlisle and his short temper. She couldn't imagine him taking time to talk to one of his horses.

She thought of Camilla and her superior ways, of the gleamingly clinical stable yard at Rychester, of the fierce argument she had heard between Amy and Jasper earlier.

"Oh, it's brilliant," she said finally. "Everybody's really nice there."

"Good." Nick smiled down at her. "I'm glad it's working out for you Jess. Although we all miss you at Sandy Lane of course."

Jess was silent. She hadn't know that. Not really. She had hoped it was true, but to hear Nick say it...

Suddenly she was engulfed by an enormous wave of sorrow and regret. I miss Sandy Lane too! she wanted to cry out. But she couldn't say that now, not after she had just told Nick how brilliant everything was. Suddenly Jess didn't want to hang about any more. She didn't want to smile brightly and answer the inevitable questions about Rychester that her friends would be bound to ask on returning from their ride.

"I have to go," she said quickly to Nick. "Will you tell everyone I said hello, and I'll see them soon?"

Nick nodded and Jess gave Storm Cloud a pat goodbye. Waving to Nick, she mounted Skylark and began the ride back to Rychester.

As she walked Skylark along the winding country lanes, she thought about Nick and Stormy, and about Sandy Lane too. Then she thought about Skylark and Rychester.

"I should be the happiest girl in the world, Skylark," she said to her pony. "I've got you and we're jumping in a really good competition soon and I'm part of the smartest riding school around. So why do I feel so miserable?" But of course, Skylark didn't reply.

As they clattered back into the yard at Rychester, Jess felt strangely empty. Wearily she slipped down from Skylark's saddle. But suddenly here was Camilla, striding towards her. "It's a good job you're always so keen on untacking Skylark yourself," Camilla said crossly.

"What do you mean?" Jess asked.

"Well, Amy's not around to do it any more," Camilla announced. "Daddy's gone and sacked her."

12

JESS HAS DOUBTS

Jess didn't feel as comfortable riding at Rychester any more. With Amy gone the stables took on a different feel. Amy's replacement, a sour-faced girl called Mel, was hard and unhelpful. Amy had always had an encouraging word for Jess or an easy smile. Jess missed her friendly face. No one seemed to know where she had gone to, although Jess had asked.

One day the postman pulled up at the stables with a registered package addressed to Amy. Jess was the only one around at the time and, as she turned the package over in her hands, she noted the sender's name – Barry Watkins. Why did that sound familiar?

She shrugged. "I'm sorry, I can't help you," she said to the postman. "Amy's moved on and no one seems to know where she's gone."

"Oh well." The postman took the package and went off whistling.

Meanwhile, lessons for Ash Hill continued apace, and Jasper, when he wasn't at work, made sure he was in attendance to give his opinions. Martin Jennings was still training them once a week, but now Mel was around as well, adding her opinion. She always backed Jasper up so that any criticism felt doubly harsh.

The Ash Hill team were all capable riders but, anxious to get into Jasper's good books, an uneasy feeling of competitiveness had crept its way between them. Only Camilla seemed oblivious to it all. She was her father's daughter when it came to her obsession with success. All her talk was of winning this show, or that show, of how Apollo was bound to jump really well at Ash Hill and bring home a load of rosettes for Rychester. Jess hoped so too, but Skylark's winning potential wasn't the only reason she loved her pony.

"I wish you'd get your act together, Jess," Camilla snorted after one particularly bad lesson the Saturday before the show. Skylark had refused twice and finally run out at the second to last fence. "I'm beginning to think you'll be more of a liability than an asset at Ash Hill."

Jess was furious. "Skylark and I would be fine if people like you and your dad would lay off us for a while."

Camilla shrugged in an off-hand manner. "Fair enough. But if Apollo showed me up like that, I would think about selling him on."

"Selling him on?" Jess gasped in disbelief. "But Camilla, you... you couldn't part with him, he's perfect."

"The only perfect ponies are prize-winning ponies,"

Camilla said airily. "That's what Daddy always says."

Jess heard that message again the same afternoon when Jasper met her as she walked Skylark across the stable yard.

"Off for a spot of jumping?" he demanded, stopping Jess in her tracks.

"No, I think we've jumped enough times this week." Jess climbed into the saddle. "I was going to take Skylark out for a hack." Jess was nervous, but determined. She wouldn't let Jasper bully her.

"I don't think that's such a good idea," Jasper said sternly. "You should be cramming in the jumping practice, you know. I hope you realize, Jess, that all the horses at Rychester have won plenty of competitions before. Skylark's the only one without a rosette for us yet. And remember Jess, a perfect pony is a prize-winning one. There's only room for winners in my stables."

Jess waited for him to smile in jest – he couldn't be serious could he? But with that, Jasper was gone.

Jess looked after him in stunned silence. What was he saying? That Skylark wasn't any good because she hadn't won anything yet? Jess was amazed that anyone could be so heartless. She shivered. Sometimes Jasper's words frightened her.

****

"Oh Jess, she's fantastic. A real dream to ride." Rosie grinned broadly at Jess as she drew Skylark to a halt at the edge of the field.

Jess leaned forward in Minstrel's saddle and smiled back at Rosie. "She's lovely, isn't she?" And then as Minstrel snorted loudly, Jess laughed and patted the piebald's shaggy neck. "You're lovely too, Minstrel – in a riding school type of way!"

"Speaking of which," Rosie said reluctantly. "We ought to head back to Sandy Lane. It's getting late."

As the two girls rode the ponies across the fields towards Sandy Lane, Jess felt happy – really happy – for the first time in ages. The Wednesday evening light was fading and soon she would have to head back to Rychester to stable Skylark. In the meantime, it had been excellent to share her new pony with Rosie at last. And it had been comforting to ride Minstrel again, whose familiar gait and steady ways inspired a nostalgic feeling for her old stables.

As they clattered into Sandy Lane, they saw Tom leading Chancey into his stable. He gave Jess and Rosie a friendly wave as he went. Alex and Kate, who were arguing over who's turn it was to sweep the yard, looked up and greeted Jess.

"Skylark's lovely, Jess, you lucky thing," Charlie called as he unchained his bike.

Jess tethered Skylark to the yard rail and followed Rosie into Minstrel's stable to untack the pony.

"We've been really busy training for the Ash Hill show," Rosie said conversationally as they worked. "How are Rychester doing?"

"Oh, they're all pretty determined," Jess said quickly. She didn't feel much like talking about

Rychester at the moment. She was more interested in Sandy Lane. "What's the news here then?" she asked her friend.

"Oh, the usual, I suppose," Rosie paused.

"Tell me the usual," Jess urged.

"OK, well, Storm Cloud's still lame, but the vet's coming to check her in the next few days," Rosie began. "And Izzy and I have been practising for Ash Hill together. Pepper and Midnight get on well, so we always try to ride together after school... mind you, we're not very disciplined about it. Izzy's so funny, we always end up having a laugh. Nick gets cross with us. He says Ash Hill's going to be a challenging show and it's the focused and determined riders who'll do best, but we're just having fun really. Um, what else?" Rosie slipped off Minstrel's bridle. "Oh yes, there's a little girl just started lessons. Her name's Hannah. Anyway, she adores Minstrel and has been spoiling him rotten – loading him up with sugar lumps. Minstrel thinks it's brilliant. He's devoted to her."

Rosie chattered away excitedly, and Jess felt a pang of envy. They didn't need her here at all. Well, it didn't matter. She had Skylark and that was all that counted, wasn't it?

"Oh and listen to this, Jess," Rosie continued. "Nick's having all his Ash Hill riders round for supper on Friday after school. It's sort of to say thanks to all the regulars really. There's been loads of extra work to do here – tons of horribly muddy ponies to groom and leaky stables to clear out and Nick says we've all really pulled our weight and he's proud of us and, oh..." Rosie stopped short as she caught sight of Jess's mournful expression.

"It's all right, Rosie." Jess gave a little shrug. "I know I'm not a Sandy Lane regular anymore. It sounds as if you're all having a lot of fun."

"Well..." Rosie sounded apologetic. "It's been all right. Probably nowhere near as exciting as the things you've been doing. We've all missed you Jess, but you're the lucky one, having Skylark and being able to keep her at Rychester. I mean, it's top of the range!"

"Nothing but the best for Jasper Carlisle," Jess muttered under her breath.

But Rosie, turning to adjust Minstrel's haynet, appeared not to have heard her.

13

REVELATIONS

"Is this that horse show you're entered for on Saturday?" Jess's brother, Jack, rustled the pages of the *Daily Advertiser* and laughed heartily. "Ooh, listen to this," he read aloud.

"The Ash Hill Show will be officially opened at 11 o'clock by Prunella Goldes, lovely star of the hit television series *Horses For Courses*. I quite fancy her actually. Think I might come and have a look at this pony show of yours after all."

"You're revolting, Jack," Jess snorted in disgust. "Here, give me that paper. I want to have a look." She grabbed the *Daily Advertiser* from her brother, who stayed slouched in his armchair.

"Hey give that back!" Jack called feebly, but Jess wouldn't listen to him and soon he left the room.

Transfixed, Jess stared at the front page of the paper. For a horrible moment the Ash Hill Show faded into insignificance as her eyes followed the lead story. *'Proof of Animal Testing at Lab of Shame'* the headline screamed, and then in smaller letters, *'by Penny Webster'*.

As Jess read on with mounting horror, familiar names leapt out and grabbed her by the throat.

'*Vrai Vert Cosmetics has long prided itself on its cruelty-free beauty products,"* the column read. *"Brands such as Mango Miracle Shampoo and Essence of Peach Perfume are household names. Part of their popularity derives from the company claiming that none of their products is tested on animals. Now an unnamed source has revealed that animals were routinely used for testing during the redevelopment of the company's bestselling Mango Miracle Shampoo, recently re-launched as New Improved Mango Miracle Shampoo. Vrai Vert Cosmetics' Managing Director, Jasper Carlisle, a local man and owner of the county's renowned Rychester Riding Stables, was unavailable for comment yesterday.'*

The piece continued for a few more paragraphs but Jess couldn't read any more. Her head ached and she felt a stab of pain as she remembered Camilla's words – 'Daddy set up Rychester with the profits from his cosmetics company'.

Amy and Jasper's cross words in the tack room swam about Jess's head:

'What have you told the press about me?'

'Why? Have you got something to hide?'

Did Amy know about all this? Was she Penny Webster's 'unnamed source?' There were so many things that Jess didn't understand. The one thing she was sure of was that animal testing was horribly cruel and unnecessary. Jess put her head in her hands.

"I don't understand any of this," she wailed aloud.

"What is there to understand, Jess?" Her mother's voice was concerned but distracted as she walked into the room, automatically picking up discarded clothes as she went. "Honestly, I wish you kids would clean up after yourselves. How many times do I have to tell you to hang your coats up when you come in?"

Jess folded the newspaper quickly and tried to slide it under the table. Her parents had seemed happy about her having a pony – the last thing she wanted was for her mother to start asking questions about Rychester. If anything went wrong with Rychester, what would happen about the free stabling for Skylark? She couldn't bear to contemplate that now. But her mother had seen her hide the paper.

She shook her head. "I've seen that article on Jasper's company."

"It's not going to mean anything bad for Rychester, is it Mum?" Jess asked earnestly.

"I don't know what it will mean for the stables," her mother replied slowly. "But if the story's true, then I think Jasper's probably broken some kind of advertising law. Take that shampoo for instance. I know the label clearly says it hasn't been tested on animals. It could be quite serious for Jasper if that's found out to be untrue."

Jess looked horrified. When the phone rang a few moments later, she was in too much of a daze to realize at first that her mother was beckoning to her.

"It's Rosie for you, Jess," her mother said, holding the outstretched receiver. Still deep in thought, Jess took the phone and heard her friend's excited voice on the other end of the line.

"Jess, have you seen the paper? That piece about Jasper Carlisle? What a horrible man he must be to let animals be used for cruel experiments!"

"Yes," Jess said slowly. "I've just read it." She thought of the times she had raved about Rychester to Rosie and bit her tongue with embarrassment. But she couldn't admit that she had been wrong.

"Look, we don't even know if the paper's story is true yet, Rosie," Jess said quickly now. "Let's not be quick to judge."

At the other end of the phone, Rosie remained silent for a moment and then, with her voice carefully controlled, spoke again. "You're right, Jess. It might all be some awful mistake. So anyway, have you done that English homework yet? I thought the comprehension was really hard..."

14

DILEMMA

Rychester Stables was buzzing with the story in the *Daily Advertiser* as Jess arrived there the next morning.

"Don't mention that article around Daddy," Camilla hissed at Jess when she walked across the yard. "He's absolutely furious. He says he's going to sue that Penny Webster for all the things she said."

"It isn't true then?" Jess asked, hopefully. She desperately wanted it to be some kind of terrible mistake.

Camilla laughed sneeringly. "Honestly Jess," she scoffed. "Do you believe everything you read in the papers? Anyway, it's clear who it was who concocted the fairy story. Daddy's convinced it was Amy. She's obviously just trying to get back at him because he sacked her. Well it's about time you knew, Jess, Amy was lazy and her work was shoddy. Daddy had no choice but to let her go. Anyway, I'm not going to talk about this any more."

And with that, Camilla was gone. Jess's mind was in a whirl. Camilla was so sure of herself, so certain she – or rather, her father Jasper – was in the right. But Jess wasn't satisfied. She knew Amy wasn't lazy. It was Camilla who could never be bothered to untack or groom Apollo after a lesson. Amy always did that for her. And Jess had never seen any evidence of shoddy work. Camilla was lying. Jasper couldn't have sacked Amy for bad work. Why then had he sacked her? And why would Amy make up a story for the papers? It didn't make sense.

Jess took a deep breath. She walked slowly across the yard towards Skylark's box.

"Yes Mrs. Jones." She heard Jasper saying on the telephone as she passed the office. "I'm so sorry Julia feels she no longer wishes to ride here. The piece in the paper was most unfortunate and, I'm afraid, completely mistaken, but I'm sure we could work this out over a drink at my house... all right. I'll speak to you soon. Tell Gerald we must get together for that game of golf sometime..."

Jess hurried on. She slid into Skylark's loose box.

"We'll just get today's jumping lesson over with, Skylark," she whispered. "Nothing's going to spoil Ash Hill for us, but things just don't feel right around here anymore."

Skylark gave a little snort. Jess smiled weakly. "What's that Skylark? Are you saying you didn't think they ever did?"

****

"I want you all to concentrate at Ash Hill tomorrow. We've got some serious jumping to do and a trophy to win," Jasper laughed as the lesson came to an end.

Jess stroked Skylark's nose gently and felt uncomfortable. She still hadn't decided whether she believed the story in the papers or not, and thinking about Ash Hill wasn't exciting for Jess any more. She felt empty... hollow.

Jess looked at her other team-mates. None of them had ridden well, and Samantha's face was pale and drawn. She seemed nervous and tense, as if she was already thinking about what would happen if she failed to win anything tomorrow. Allison was looking sullen and even the normally lively Lucy was kicking the ground miserably with her heels. Only Camilla appeared unconcerned, and Jess wasn't surprised. Camilla was an excellent rider, she was bound to do well for Rychester. But then again, Jess wasn't sure what emotions her imperious face was masking.

"OK, we'll call it a day for now," Jasper said. "We'll meet here tomorrow morning at 7 o'clock sharp please. No dawdlers." And with that he turned smartly on his heels and was gone.

The others set about searching for Mel to untack their ponies. Jess hung back a little and watched them go. She felt detached from them. Rychester wasn't a team at all. There was no warmth or comradeship there. They were all just determined to win. Jess sighed. What was she doing here with them? Anyway, in all likelihood, Rychester was a stables that was set up with the profits from animal experiments, wasn't it? Jess felt sick. She didn't feel like taking Skylark back to her stable, not now. Jess decided she would have a quiet hack along the country lanes that led away from Rychester.

"We can clear our heads, Skylark," she said. "Think things through a bit."

She trotted Skylark out of the stable yard and down the winding lane. As she turned the bend she almost bumped into a girl walking quickly along the grass verge before she recognized her. At the last moment, Jess drew Skylark up and gave a cry of surprise.

"Amy!" What are you doing around here?"

"Hello Jess." Amy smiled up at her, startled but friendly. "I'm working over at Southdown Stables now. I just came back to pick up some things I'd left in the tack room at Rychester." She held up a bag.

"But Jasper," Jess began slowly. "Did he see you? He's really cross with you, you know."

"Frightened more like," Amy replied grimly. "No, I took a chance while you were having a lesson. I crept in and out quickly. Did you see the article in the paper then?"

"Yes, we all did," Jess said. She slipped down from the saddle and slipped the reins over Skylark's neck as the pony bent down to graze at the verge. "What's going on Amy? Is it true what Penny Webster wrote? And why did Jasper sack you? It's not because your work was bad, is it?"

Amy laughed. "That's a lot of questions, Jess. OK, first of all, whatever you might have heard, Jasper didn't sack me. I resigned. Jasper's way of doing things just made me uncomfortable. He was pushing everyone too hard. He didn't really care about the horses at all. I think that was obvious to everyone. He's just in it for the glory they can bring to him. I couldn't handle his obsession with success, with winning."

Amy paused and Jess was silent. She knew in her heart that what Amy was saying was true. Jess had to admit that Rychester wasn't the kind of stables she had hoped it would be. And that had everything to do with Jasper. He had charmed and flattered her at first, told her she was a plucky rider and Skylark was a spirited pony. But he had also been bullying and sometimes threatening.

"I overheard part of an argument between you and Jasper one day in the tack room," Jess confessed now. "Something about the press."

"Ah yes, the final straw." Amy smiled. "That was all a bit of a coincidence really. My cousin Barry was working as a technician at the Vrai Vert Cosmetics Laboratory. The company were re-launching their *Mango Miracle Shampoo* and he told me that quite a lot of animal testing had taken place during the new product trials. It's all a bit complicated, but basically it means that Jasper's advertising slogan was a lie – you know the 'Caring Cosmetics Company'." Amy stopped to draw breath, and Jess waited anxiously for her to start again.

"Anyway, I was so fed up at Rychester that I ended up mentioning it to Penny Webster. Oh, that's right–" Amy paused as she remembered. "I think you interrupted our conversation one time, Jess. Anyway, Penny's never one to turn down a good story and was very interested. Surprisingly enough, what Jasper's done isn't actually illegal, but it's the kind of thing that people aren't very sympathetic to. A big public outcry could do his company's reputation a lot of damage. So now you know, Jess. It's all true."

"Oh Amy, this is awful," Jess wailed. "I've been looking forward to being at Ash Hill so much. But now it just feels all wrong – riding for Rychester I mean. What should I do?"

Amy smiled at her sympathetically and shook her head. "I think you're the only one who knows the answer to that, Jess," she said softly.

15

NIGHTMARE!

The day of the Ash Hill Show dawned bright and clear. The sunshine should have brought with it a sense of optimism, but Jess felt tired and gloomy as she cycled towards Rychester shortly after 7 o'clock. She had lain awake all night, churning things over in her mind – the things she had read in the paper, her conversation with Amy, Jasper's insistence on winning, the miserable faces of her team-mates...

Jess's legs felt like jelly as she cycled the final yards towards the stable. She knew what she had to do. As she turned into the stables, she slowed down to take in the scene. The ponies were already gathered, ready for loading into the horse boxes, and the riders all looked smart and poised. Someone had already groomed Skylark, and she stood among them, calm and serene. And then there was Jasper, standing in the middle of it all, glancing anxiously around, as though looking for someone. Jess paused and at that moment he caught sight of her.

"Jess!" he cried, pointing to his watch. "Where have you been? I hope you haven't been getting last minute nerves!"

"I'm not nervous," Jess said as she took a deep breath, "because I'm not going to ride for you today. You can win your trophies without me."

"What are you talking about?" Jasper voice was calm, dangerous even. The others all stared at Jess in amazement. "Is this some kind of bad joke, Jess?" Jasper continued. "Because this really isn't the time."

"No, it's not a joke." Jess looked at Camilla and Lucy and Samantha and Allison and suddenly she felt very certain.

"I can't ride for Rychester," she said clearly. "I don't belong with you. Skylark doesn't belong with you. You're involved with things I'm ashamed of."

Jasper laughed scornfully. "You don't believe all that rubbish in the papers do you? Come on now Jess."

"Yes," Jess said firmly. "Yes, I do believe it, so I'm not riding today. I'm not riding for Rychester ever."

"But we won't be able to win the team event without you, Jess." Camilla interrupted incredulously. "We need five riders." Her voice became wheedling. "And Skylark – she looks fantastic. She's such an asset to Rychester. All the other stables will be really envious that we've got such a good pony."

"But you haven't got her, Camilla." Jess was quietly confident. "She's my pony. Not Rychester's."

Camilla's voice changed instantly, and now she spat out her words furiously. "I always thought you were a bit of a wimp, Jess. And you're not exactly the world's greatest rider, are you? You never deserved a place on our team anyway."

Jess shrugged her shoulders and turned away. Camilla was a selfish, spoilt, girl. But then how could she help be anything but, with a father like Jasper Carlisle. Camilla's words, designed to cut, meant nothing to Jess.

"I warn you, Jess," Jasper continued. "If you leave us now, you're out of Rychester for good."

Jess walked over to her pony and put a hand on her neck. "Rychester doesn't need us, Skylark," she murmured. "So we're not going to jump today. I don't know where we're going to stable you, but we'll come up with something."

"Now just hang on a minute, Jess," Jasper's voice was cold and controlled as he took a step towards her. "Rychester may not need you, but it's certainly going to keep hold of Skylark. Do you think I wasted my time and money buying an expensive show pony just so you could whisk her off right from under my nose?"

Jess froze. What was Jasper talking about?

"You can go where you want, Jess," Jasper said now. "But Skylark belongs to Rychester, and here she will stay."

"But..." Jess was confused. She wasn't sure how to stand up to Jasper's cold aggression. Suddenly she felt very small and alone. Any boldness she might have felt before evaporated slowly. "But Skylark's mine," she said. "I won her."

"Legally Skylark is still Rychester's," Jasper said. "For the year she's stabled here anyway. It was part of the competition rules... you can't have read the small print properly. Now, if you'll excuse me, we've got a show to win... Mel!" Jasper called loudly as the stable girl appeared. "Let's get these horses into the box. You'll be riding Skylark for Rychester today."

Could it be true? Jess didn't know what to say. She stood rooted to the spot, looking helplessly on as Skylark was led up the ramp of the box. There was nothing she could do to stop her pony being taken away. As the box roared out of the stable yard, she could only stare after it. What had she done? If only she had kept her mouth shut and stuck with Rychester, she wouldn't be in this position now and Skylark would still be hers.

In a flash Jess knew what she had to do next and, grabbing her bike, she flew out of the Rychester yard without a backward glance. Pedalling furiously along the country lanes, she didn't stop for breath until she arrived, twenty minutes later, at Sandy Lane Stables. The familiar homely yard was bustling with activity as riders and horses prepared for the Ash Hill Show. Suddenly shy, Jess pedalled slowly up the drive.

A puzzled Rosie looked up from where she was plaiting Pepper's mane and stared straight at Jess. Then her face broke into a beaming smile and she rushed over to her friend.

"Jess, what are you doing here? I thought we'd be seeing you at Ash Hill. We're just getting ready to go. Where's Skylark?"

"Jess!" Charlie cried. "Where have you been hiding?"

"Hello Jess," Tom smiled at her. "Been jumping any more death traps recently?"

It was all too much. The sound of her friends' voices, alongside her anxiety about Skylark caused something inside Jess to snap, and suddenly she could hold the tears back no longer...

"Jess... Jess. What is it?" Nick appeared and his face showed only concern as he tried to console the girl. "Take a deep breath and start at the beginning," he started, leading her off to the cottage.

Jess managed to take control of herself, telling Nick everything that had happened – the story in the paper, her decision not to ride at Ash Hill, how she had gone about telling Jasper, and finally about Skylark not really being hers.

Nick sighed heavily and shook his head. "What a story, Jess," he said seriously. "Jasper Carlisle sounds like a nasty piece of work. But I'm proud of you. For what it's worth, I think you've made the right decision."

"I thought I had to," Jess squeaked miserably. "But what about Skylark? It looks as though I've lost her."

Nick fiddled with some pens on the table and glanced out of the window at the others getting ready for Ash Hill in the stable yard. He seemed to be weighing things up in his mind and it was a few minutes before he spoke again. When he did, his voice was measured.

"Look, I don't know all the fine details about this competition," he said slowly. "But I'll go and talk to Jasper this evening. I'll think things through at the show, but right now, we have to be on our way. Make sure you're here at 6 o'clock this evening and we'll drive over to Rychester."

Jess's heart leapt hopefully, but she was still upset. "Can't I come with you to the Ash Hill Show?" she pleaded.

"I know it's difficult, Jess," Nick shook his head.

"But it's probably best if you stay away from the show today. It might be awkward if Jasper sees you there, and I don't want any scenes. Let's wait and tackle him tonight. Trust me on this one, OK?" Nick put a comforting hand on Jess's shoulder.

Jess was desperate to go to Ash Hill, frantic to see Skylark, but Nick had asked her to trust him and she would. As she followed Nick out of the tack room into the stable yard, Rosie raised her eyebrows enquiringly, but Jess had no time to talk to her because Nick had taken charge.

"Come on everybody," he called now. "Let's get these horses loaded or we'll be late."

And for the second time that morning, Jess was left standing on her own in a stable yard, watching as a horse box drove away to Ash Hill. As this one disappeared out of sight, Jess looked downcast and kicked her heels in the gravelled earth. It was going to be a long day. She'd told her parents she hadn't been picked to ride at Ash Hill, but they still thought she was going along to watch. She could hardly just turn up at home – that would mean explaining everything. And she didn't want to tell them all that yet. She knew they would only worry about what she was going to do with Skylark. No, she'd just have to busy herself around Sandy Lane.

Jess wandered over to the cottage and found Nick's wife, Sarah, tucked away in the cosy kitchen of the cottage.

"Jess!" Sarah looked surprised to see her. "What are you doing here?"

"It's a bit of a long story," Jess answered wearily.

"Well, sit down and tell me everything." Sarah

beckoned to the table. "Have you had breakfast yet?"

"No." Jess shook her head, suddenly realizing that she was very hungry.

"Good, well there's a basket of croissants that need eating up before Ebony slobbers all over them." Sarah smiled. "And then I was planning to lunge Storm Cloud. I could do with some help..."

"Count me in." Jess beamed broadly.

16

SHOWDOWN

At a quarter to six that evening, Jess stood in the yard at Sandy Lane, impatiently waiting for everyone to get back from the show. She had been home for a quick supper, but hadn't told her parents about the events of the day.

At six on the dot, the horse box rolled up the drive and the yard was immediately a flurry of activity.

"Jess... Jess," Rosie cried. "I won... Pepper and I won the Open Jumping."

"The Open Jumping? That's brilliant." Jess was delighted for her friend. "And where was Rychester?"

"Nowhere," Rosie grinned. "Not a rosette in sight... they fell to pieces. The team event was won by a stables on the other side of Brookwood. You should have seen Jasper Carlisle's face... he was red with rage."

"Really?" Jess laughed with surprise. She couldn't quite believe what Rosie had told her. Surely at least

Camilla would have won something. But there wasn't time to ask questions now as Nick was running back out of the cottage.

"Sorry Jess, I had to make a phone call. All part of the plan." He smiled at her mysteriously as he opened the door of the Land Rover. "Right, are you ready to go?"

Jess could only nod. What had Nick got in store? What was he planning to say to Jasper?

As if sensing her unease, Nick kept up a steady stream of chatter on the way to Rychester. Jess listened silently, grateful that he didn't seem to need any response from her.

"Rosie and Pepper jumped tremendously, Jess," Nick said. "You would have been proud of her. The competition from Rychester wasn't very fierce after all. Who was the rather sour-faced girl riding Skylark? It was so funny – she pounded your poor pony into the ring and launched her at the first jump on far too tight a rein–"

Jess winced at this, but Nick hadn't finished the story.

"Skylark wasn't having any of it and screeched to a halt in front of the fence. The girl went soaring over the top and landed very unceremoniously on her bottom. Skylark was completely unfazed and just stood there shaking her head and neighing loudly. They retired of course." Nick shook his head and smiled. Jess couldn't stop herself from laughing out loud.

They were still laughing as the Land Rover turned into the drive at Rychester. The place looked deserted and suddenly Jess felt herself tense up. What if Jasper wasn't here? What if he'd already taken Skylark away somewhere else? She jumped down from the cab and ran over to her pony's loose box. Her heart leapt with joy as she saw Skylark poking her head curiously over the stable door. The grey pony gave a loud whinny as Jess reached up and hugged her neck. She breathed a sigh of relief. So far, so good.

Jess turned around and saw Nick striding over to the office. Quickly she ran over as he was knocking on the door.

"Come in." Jasper's voice came loud and clear.

Jess followed Nick into the office. Jasper sat at the desk, rifling through some papers on the table in front of him. He was alone. When he saw Nick walking towards him, he jumped up.

"Hello, can I help?" he asked.

Nick put out his hand and smiled politely. "I don't think we've met," he said evenly. "I'm Nick Brooks. I own Sandy Lane Stables over at Colcott."

"Sandy Lane. Where have I heard that name recently?" Jasper said. And then he caught sight of Jess, standing nervously behind Nick, and his friendly voice didn't sound quite so friendly any more.

"You've got a nerve showing your face around here, haven't you?" he said.

"Er, it's actually Skylark we've come about, Mr. Carlisle," Nick said, interrupting Jasper mid-flow before the conversation could get heated. Quickly he went on before Jasper had a chance to say anything. "I understand Jess isn't able to keep Skylark here any more, so I've offered to keep the pony at Sandy Lane. We've come to collect her and settle any outstanding bills."

Jess gave a gasp and her stomach churned excitedly.

Keep Skylark at Sandy Lane? It was an excellent plan, but would Jasper allow it? As she looked at Jasper and saw the malicious grin spread across his face, she realized Nick was clearly mistaken if he thought it was going to be that simple.

Jasper let out a low, disbelieving laugh. "Very good of you Mr. Brooks," he started, his silvery voice still sounding pleasant. "Who wouldn't want a pony as valuable as Skylark? But I'm afraid it's not quite as easy as that." Jasper put his hand into the top drawer of his desk and drew out some official looking papers. "You see Skylark legally belongs to Rychester."

And as he handed the papers to Nick to look at, he spoke again. "If any of you had bothered to read the rules you would have seen that," he said, flashing the briefest of smiles. "And by entering the competition, Jess, you gave your agreement to abide by those rules," he explained rather smugly.

Jess felt suddenly faint and the room began to spin. She took a deep breath and looked around her. The tables and chairs, the filing cabinets, Nick and Jasper, they seemed to disappear somewhere far away and all she was aware of was the pounding of her heart and the sound of her breathing. Everything else had gone very quiet. So this was it. Her dream really was over. Skylark wasn't hers.

"Is that some kind of threat?" Jasper's angry voice cut through her thoughts and she looked up to see him looking angrily at Nick. What was going on? What had Nick said? Jasper looked furious, but Nick was calm. He shook his head slowly and when he spoke again his voice was reasonable.

"Not at all, Mr. Carlisle," Nick said. "It's just an

observation. I would have thought that with all the trouble your cosmetics company is in at the moment, the last thing you need is bad publicity about your riding stables."

What was Nick talking about? Jess listened hard.

"I shouldn't think taking away a child's pony will add anything to your already damaged reputation," Nick said seriously.

"But the pony's mine," Jasper spat.

"*Carlisle the Pony Snatcher*," a familiar voice rang out from the office door and everyone turned around to see Penny Webster from the *Daily Advertiser* standing on the doorstep.

"What...?" Jasper began.

"Hello everybody," Penny smiled as she walked cooly into the room. "Thanks for the phone call, Mr. Brooks. You're right – the *Daily Advertiser* would be very interested in the story. Now let me see if I've got the facts straight," Penny paused dramatically and flicked through her notebook. "*Jasper Carlisle, owner of the disgraced cosmetics company, Vrai Vert, gives a pony away in a competition,*" she continued. "*But when the lucky winner decides, understandably, after all that has happened, that she doesn't want to keep her pony on at Rychester, Mr. Carlisle surprises her with the announcement that the pony isn't really hers at all.* Some mean trick to play on a child, don't you think? I can see the story on the front page of tomorrow's *Daily Advertiser* accompanied by a picture of the tearful child." Penny glanced sympathetically at Jess.

"All right, all right." Jasper held up his hand. "I can see you've got this all worked out." His voice became quieter. "Have the pony. It disgraced me at Ash Hill today anyway. It's more trouble than it's worth. Just take it away from here and–"

"We'll say no more about it?" Nick said enquiringly.

"Yes, all right," Jasper spluttered. He sank down into his chair, and Jess noticed the lines on his face. He suddenly looked very old. He clearly wasn't used to not getting his own way. "Now get out of here, the lot of you." Jasper pointed wearily at the door.

"If you could just sign here." Nick pointed to a space on the documents, then there's no problem, we'll be quite happy to take the pony off your hands."

With a grimace, Jasper signed away, and Jess, Nick and Penny needed no second bidding. As the office door shut behind them and they emerged into the stable yard, Nick turned to Penny. "Thanks for turning up here," he smiled. "I don't think Mr. Carlisle would have given in without you."

"That's OK," Penny said. "I'm glad things have turned out the way they have." Penny flashed Jess a smile.

"Now how are we going to get you and Skylark back to Sandy Lane then?" Nick turned to Jess with a sparkle in his eye. "You won't both fit in the Land Rover."

Jess grinned back. She wanted to thank Nick, but she was speechless with happiness.

"Well, her tack's still here, I presume," Nick continued as Jess nodded silently.

"In that case," Nick said. "There's only one thing to do."

"I'll have to ride her back to Sandy Lane," Jess finished, finding her voice at last.

"What a good idea," Nick said. "I'll head off now and get her stable ready."

"Thanks Nick... thanks for everything," Jess managed, before she raced off to get Skylark.

17

HOME AT LAST

Jess leaned back on her brush the next day and surveyed the stable yard. Stray bits of hay blew across the ground and there was no denying the woodwork on the buildings could do with a lick of paint. But to Jess, Sandy Lane Stables looked perfect. Skylark too seemed happy enough in the small but snug spare loose box.

Jess had explained everything to her parents when she'd got home yesterday evening – about Jasper trying to keep Skylark, and Nick's part in the pony's recovery. Her parents had been appalled at the story and then worried... worried how they were ever going to be able to pay Nick back for the stabling. But Jess had soon told them everything – how Nick had offered to keep Skylark at livery in return for her use in lessons, and how she didn't mind that – not when it meant she got to keep her pony.

"Well that's a relief," her mother had said at the end of Jess's long explanations.

And for Jess, the arrangement was perfect.

Now, Skylark stood looking out over the stable door, as Rosie cycled into the yard.

"Hi Jess." Rosie waved.

"Rosie... at last!" Jess grinned and walked over to her friend. "Now we've got time to talk... so what went on at Ash Hill? Whatever did happen to the Rychester girls?" she asked. "They'd been practising so hard. I can't believe they didn't do very well... although it's brilliant you won... and of course I didn't doubt for a moment you were in with a chance for the trophy," she added quickly.

Rosie beamed with delight. "Well thanks Jess. I must admit, I was rather worried about the Rychester riders in the individual competition, but they completely fell to pieces when it came down to it. They'd all been arguing so much before the event that they didn't know if they were coming or going. Only one of them was placed – a girl called Samantha."

"Oh yes, I rode with her at Rychester," Jess answered. "In fact, I bumped into her in town the other day. She didn't tell me much though. Do you know what happened to Camilla Carlisle?" Jess asked urgently.

"Well, you should have seen her," Rosie chortled. "She *really* lost her rag. I heard her arguing with her dad just before she was about to go into the ring. I suppose that's what really did it for her. She was all fired up... completely lost her composure and I don't think her palomino liked being hauled about one bit... refused three times at the wall, and almost bucked her off too."

"Good for Apollo," Jess laughed. "I wonder if Jasper will throw Camilla out of Rychester for not winning. Look, why don't we get a drink in the tack room before the others arrive?"

"Good idea," Rosie said. "Have you seen today's paper, Jess?"

"No, what's in it?" Jess was puzzled.

"I'll show you," Rosie smiled.

In the small and cosy tack room, Rosie and Jess huddled into worn easy chairs. Rosie spread the *Daily Advertiser* out on the table.

"Look!" Rosie stabbed at an article with her finger.

'Carlisle's Comeuppance! by Penny Webster,' Jess read. *'Vrai Vert Cosmetics, who were last week exposed in these pages for lying about their animal testing procedures, are today facing more problems,'* the article continued. *'Protesters have mounted a constant vigil outside the company's laboratory in Greater Rychester. The protest organizer, Barry Watkins, said last night that they would stay until everyone in the country was aware of the company's conduct. A spokesman for the company said this will undoubtably have an effect on sales. Jasper Carlisle, owner of Vrai Vert Cosmetics was still unavailable for comment yesterday.'*

Jess sipped her juice thoughtfully. "Samantha said her dad's going to take her horse away from Rychester, and that lots of other riders are thinking of leaving. She reckons Jasper might sell up. I wonder what will happen to all those lovely ponies then?"

"Let's hope he sells the stables to someone who really cares about animals," Rosie said. "Anyway, I think we've talked enough about Rychester, don't you? Let's talk about Sandy Lane for a change! Tell me, Jess, do you mind having to lend Skylark out on rides?"

"I thought I might do at first," Jess said slowly. "But not now – Skylark will always be mine, whoever rides her." Jess drained her glass and set it down. Glancing at the clock she gave a little cry. "Yikes, Skylark's waiting, I should have tacked her up by now. See you later, Rosie."

Jess waved a hasty goodbye to her friend and grabbed Skylark's tack from the peg. Striding out into the yard she made her way to her pony's stall.

"Hello Skylark," she said as she opened the door and untethered the grey pony. "Laura Warren's going to be riding you now. But save your energy for the 11 o'clock hack with me. I bet Rosie that we'd beat her and Pepper in a race. So I hope you're ready for a good gallop!"

A Horse for the Summer by Michelle Bates

The first title in the Sandy Lane Stables series

...There was a frantic whinny and the sound of drumming hooves reverberated around the yard as Chancey pranced down the ramp. He was certainly on his toes, but he didn't look like the sleek, well turned-out horse that Tom remembered seeing last season. He was still unclipped and his shabby winter coat was flecked with foam as feverishly he pawed the ground. No one knew what to say...

When Tom is lent a prize-winning show jumper for the summer, things don't turn out quite as he'd hoped. Chancey is wild and unpredictable and Tom is forced to start training him in secret. But the days of summer are numbered and Chancey isn't Tom's to keep forever. At some point, he will have to give him back...

The Runaway Pony by Susannah Leigh

The second title in the Sandy Lane Stables series

...Angry shouting and the crunch of hooves on gravel made Jess spin around sharply. Careering towards her, wild-eyed with fear and long tail flying behind, was a palomino pony. It was completely out of control. Jess's heart began to pound and her breath came in sharp gasps, but almost without thinking she held out her arms...

When the riderless palomino pony clatters into the yard, no one is more surprised than Jess. Hot on the pony's hooves comes a man waving a head collar. Jess helps him catch the pony and sends them on their way. Little is she to know what far-reaching consequences her simple actions will have...

Strangers at the Stables by Michelle Bates

The third title in the Sandy Lane Stables series

...Thoughts jostled around in Rosie's mind as she crossed the yard. She couldn't believe how many things had gone wrong in the couple of weeks Nick and Sarah had been gone. She needed time to think. There was something worrying her, right at the back of her mind... something that held the key to it all. But what was it?

When the owners of Sandy Lane are away, everyone still expects the stables to run smoothly in their absence. No one is quite prepared for all the things that happen over the next few weeks. There isn't time to get help, the children of Sandy Lane have to act fast, if they want to save their stables...

Ride by Moonlight by Michelle Bates

The sixth title in the Sandy Lane Stables series

> The ground started spinning. Charlie's head was reeling. He felt as though he was seeing everything double. He couldn't think. He couldn't stop thinking. His mind was in a whirl as everything came flooding back – the high pitched whinny, the thundering hooves, the crashing fall – all echoed around his head...

When Charlie loses his nerve in a riding accident, no one thinks for a moment it'll be long before he's back in the saddle. But as the weeks go by, his friends begin to realize it's going to take something quite exceptional to get him riding again...